# May The HEAVEN Shine On My King

DOMENICA CALCARA

May The Heaven Shine On My King
Copyright © 2023 by Domenica Calcara

All rights reserved. No part of this publication may be reproduced, distributed, or transmitted in any form or by any means, including photocopying, recording, or other electronic or mechanical methods, without the prior written permission of the author, except in the case of brief quotations embodied in critical reviews and certain other non-commercial uses permitted by copyright law.

Tellwell Talent
www.tellwell.ca

ISBN
978-0-2288-8040-0 (Hardcover)
978-0-2288-8039-4 (Paperback)
978-0-2288-8041-7 (eBook)

# Dedication

I want to dedicate this book to my family, that have stood by me. This is for you.

# Table of Contents

Dedication ............................................................. iii
Chapter 1:   First Encounter ................................. 1
Chapter 2:   The War .............................................. 13
Chapter 3:   A Trip to France ............................... 22
Chapter 4:   Masquerade Ball ............................... 36
Chapter 5:   A New Beginning ............................. 44
Chapter 6:   A Festival ........................................... 52
Chapter 7:   Three Weddings ............................... 57
Chapter 8:   A New Member Arrives ................... 65
Chapter 9:   The Next Generation ........................ 71
Chapter 10: A New Life .......................................... 74
Chapter 11: A New Beginning for Prince Elias ...... 80
Chapter 12: A Big Surprise .................................... 89
Acknowledgments ................................................ 101
Last word from the Author .................................. 103
Note from the Author .......................................... 105

# Chapter 1

## First Encounter

King Walt got off his horse and saw Margery from afar. His heart and soul knew she was the one. Heartful face as she walked through the fields. He knew he had to do something about it, he followed her for days to make sure if she showed up at the same spot and she did. On a beautiful sunny morning, he stopped his horse right in front of her. He had a smile that you want to smile too. She smiled with her beautiful green eyes, and he knew she was interested. He asked her if she would like to take a walk one day near his castle and she agreed. She walked back to her chambers and decided to call her chamber ladies to help her choose something nice to wear. She ended up choosing a blue dress. Her long blond hair almost to her waist and a beautiful necklace around her neck. She was ready for the meeting between her and the King. He came on his beautiful horse and waited there right in front of her grand staircase. And as she appeared at the staircase, his eyes met hers and it was the beginning of something grand. The horses were waiting for them, and he said "Margery, give me your hand and I'll lift you up on your horse." All day they rode on their horses, side by side through the fields of green grass right under their feet. The wind blowing lightly and the sun shining in their faces. Walt bends his head towards her, smiled, and said "You look beautiful today". Remembering the moment when he said, "Give me your hand and I'll lift you on your horse". "Walt you're very good at riding." "Yes, I know I've been riding since I was five." Let's go through the bushes upon the top of the hill where you can see my castle. "Do you see it?" "Yes, it's great" Come, and I'll let the servants cook us a meal. Henrietta and Cassandra prepared Margery and I something delicious. Cassandra and Henrietta started cooking in the kitchen. The kitchen started to smell wonderful. While Walt and Margery wondered through the halls. Margery said, "What a beautiful staircase all in white, it takes your breath away". He touched her hand and it led to the terrace facing the grounds in a spectacular view. As I'm standing holding onto the mantle, I feel the breeze pass through me and it's telling me that King Walt is the man for me. He touches my hand and says, "I know we've just met here. I want to be with you for the rest of my life." The King said. She almost lost her balance and she whispered "Yes." Margery was looking at his face and a tear ran down his face "You are the love of my life." Margery replied. The King smiled and said, "I've chosen a date February 25. How does that sound?" she replied "Wonderful." The wedding dress shall have red and gold all around and you'll have beautiful shoes as well. And a surprise from me. On that day. Tears flowed down my face and his soft hand touched my face. That touch will last me a lifetime. We left the grounds just in time before the rain started to fall on us. Like sprinkles of falling stars. We arrived just in time just before for it started to pour. "From now on I'll start the preparations." He turned around and left. Come morning I decided to go hunting with my fellow men. As we gathered our horses and tided our boots, we climbed onto our horses. "Come men I have a spot where to go for hunting." said the King. Michael one of his 1st officers asked him, "Let's catch as much food for supper tonight." "Yes, Michael we'll do our best to catch as many as we can." said the King. We rode our horses through the mud with the mud splashing unto us. As we rode, the wind blowing through us. And we passed through the fields like thunder. We stopped and climbed off our horses and started shooting for game. Michael shot 3 pheasants, I shot 4 and 2nd officer Jonah shot 3, and Jax and

Marcus got 3 also. "Come men let's regroup, let's attach the game to our horses and be on our way." Riding back, we heard shots in the forest just above us. We saw two men on the floor, one was wounded the other was hurt badly. "Men what happened?" said the King. "We got into a fight." "Do you need our services? Come with us." We'll help you get back on your feet men, carry them on our horses. We rode back to the castle and my men brought the wounded in. "Henrietta and Cassandra, get food for the wounded." "Give them a warm meal and once they're ready, let them be on their way." the King said, "Call upon me before they leave so I may give them something for their return home." After two days of recovering, they received some money from the King and those men went on their way. "King!" One of those men said, "Thanks for helping us we will never forget the kindness you showed unto us". the King said, "It's nothing" That afternoon, he rested on his bed, tired from the morning ride, and he fell asleep. When he woke up, he made his way to the kitchen and asked the cooks to prepare a roast for dinner. He called upon Margery to join him for dinner. The dining reception hall was laid out for the evening. White linens in gold lace. He was dressed in his black jacket that made him look handsome. As he came in, he asked Margery to sit down. "Let's talk about the wedding plans. who will be coming." said the King. Then Margery answered, "my family and my closest relatives that's all." "I will invite all the court of course." said the King. The roast from the other room smelled amazing. Once it came to us, I couldn't wait to eat into it. As we ate and drank, and Jax walked in, Good looking man with his men on his side and his two fellow comrades. "Sire! Do you need us tonight? Or can we go out with my comrades." "No, you are dismissed for the night." The King said. "Jonah, Marcus, Giacomo, let's go to the tavern." said Jax. The men walked out of the dining area and started to walk down cobble stone streets. We walked at the tavern. They pushed the door in and I sat at a table, where they could see over the fields. At the dining room, while me and Walt are dining, my heart was startled for I felt the same way my King. "I love you forever." Walt raised his cup and told Margery, "May we have many sons and daughters. I LOVE YOU Margery." I had food in my mouth, I almost swallowed the whole piece of chicken. They drank their wine and walked out the door. The men noticed four ladies walking together and the men gathered their strength and asked one lady to walk with them. Jonah pulled himself together and by the end of the night, the laughter could be heard all the way down the road. Jax said, "men it's time to head back." They asked the women to see them again and they left with a courtesy. Early morning you could see the sun, shining through the window. Margery was looking forward to the walk in the open air called her ladies in waiting. "Victoria and Alexandria come to my chambers." "Let's go for a walk." they arrived at her quarters and Thea said. "Madame Margery, it's a beautiful day. Let's all go for a promenade." Victoria and Alexandria agreed. They opened the iron doors with a great force and walked out. Victoria grabbed Thea by the hand. "Come now let's go!" Alexandria grabbed both of their hands and they were laughing all the way. Margery walked in front of the girls and said, "What a beautiful day today." Little did she know that her sisters Genevieve and Melinda were coming by surprise. The castle was getting prepared for the two sisters to arrive. One was from Kent and the other was from Saxon. Both were beautiful women. Genevieve was beautiful and Melinda had a beautiful smile. Genevieve was married to Comte Vance from Saxon and Melinda was Courting Comte Fernand. While preparation we're on the way, Victoria was seen across the fields with the other ladies. "Madame Margery!" Victoria said. "Let's go back in now, it's been a nice afternoon. Let's have some tea at the dinning hall." she said. Margery agreed and told the other ladies to meet her at the dining hall. They walked in the dining hall. The cooks came in with patisserie and tea. They were waiting for us all. "They are delicious!" Thea said.

The tea was great and the patisserie were savory. Margery dismissed the ladies for the night. They headed back to their chambers to rest for the night.

The next day, Jax was so drunk from the night before. He went out with his fellow men. They had some ale at the tavern. Jax had drank too much. "Jax!" Jonah had to push him off his bed. "Come on Jax get off the bed let's go!" "The men are waiting for us." Laughing historically pulled his hand and got him up. They started at the top of the staircase running down two steps at a time. Marcus joined them running down too, come on men let's get breakfast with the king and see what our daily schedule will be. Marcus get your armor adjusted. "Let's go men." At the bottom of the staircase, we saw the King standing with his blue eyes like the ocean. "Come men we got a few things to do today." They arrived in the dining room; a beautiful spread was set. Eggs, bread, fruits, cheeses. "Sire when you're ready we'll start." Jax said. They pulled the chairs and started eating. The King asked Jax to get a hold of all his comrades because the wedding would take place in a week. Preparation had started. The King went to ask one of his close advisers to get a hold of a gold necklace with pearls on them for his bride and an initial M on it, with a Ruby clasp. Margery had planned to get her two sisters matching rings in gold with a cross on it with real stones. They were ordered and on their way to the castle. That day the Chariots arrived in front of the of the castle gate to greet Genevieve, Comte Vance, Melinda and Comte Fernand. Margery ran to the gate, hurrying to get to see her sisters. "Guards open the gate", the first carriage came Melinda arrived first with Comte Fernand and Genevieve arrived with Vance. "Hello sister. I hope life is treating you well." Melinda said. "Yes, it's been good." said Margery. "I am so happy for you." said Melinda. Genevieve got out of the carriage, and embraced her Margery and said, "I'm so happy for you." "The wedding will take place in a week." said Margery. "Come now sisters. Come Comte Vance and Comte Fernard. my servants, we'll take care of your baggage." "My sisters come, I want to show you the castle and my chambers." We walked through the halls one room at a time, until we came to the formal dining room. Blue drapes hung from beautiful windows, candles on the table. "It's splendid!" said Geneveive. She had a beautiful gown and was so beautiful walking through the halls. She was so beautiful. That soon she was going to be Queen. Everyone looked at her. "Come at my chambers" she said. There was red curtains and white silk lay on her bed. A white chest lay at the foot of the bed. Then came Melinda. I was so happy, they looked amazed. "Sister it's breathless." "I thank my King for everything." As we gathered that evening, we all dined together. As we sat and ate cooked geese on a bed of roasted potatoes with wine. Genevieve said, "it's beautiful." It was a splendid evening. The next day, the wedding ceremony was at the cathedral where all the town people gathered. At the ceremony, they exchanged these words.

⚜   ⚜   ⚜

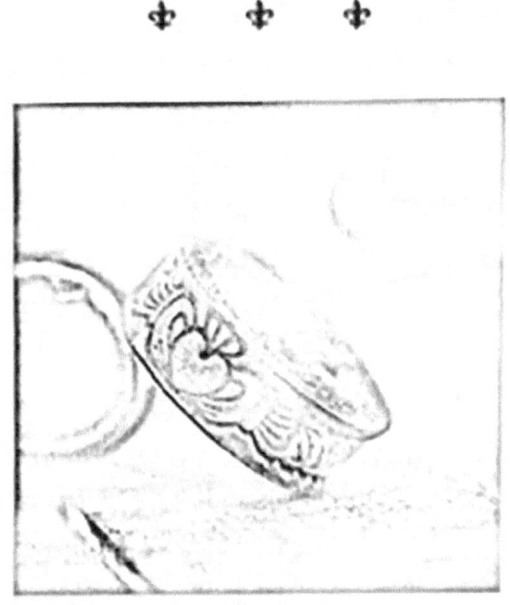

My King I Love you, you are my Life
My Queen you are my Life

The bishop handed their rings to be exchanged. They said their vows. The crowd cheered. Everyone headed that evening, to the ballroom. Everyone cheered for the King and Queen as they walked through the doors. That night, there was music and dancing, and everyone had a great evening. The next day, we walked down the corridor. We smelled fresh bread making. We smiled at each other, and it led us to the kitchen quarters, where the cooks took out of the oven the fresh bread, and Henrietta put the fresh bread on a plate with fruits just for me and Walt. We took a piece of the hot bread with oil and dipped it, it tasted great. Once we finished eating, Walt said, "come dear let's take a stroll down the corridor, before bedtime would do us good." The windows were left open so the air would come in. After dinner, I went back to my chambers. I sat and brushed my hair and stared at the moon light, "What a beautiful night my love." The King kissed my sweet forehead. The morning came and the maids came into the chambers. They filled the basin with warm water and put Jasmine oil in the warm water. I touched it with my hand and went in, once I got out of the warm basin, they dressed me with beautiful flowers on the side of my hair and braided it on both sides. The choice of dress for today was a light green that it was attached in the front. I had beautiful shoes laid out for me with diamond stones at the front and I decided to wear those for the day. Walt had done the same and was waiting for me at the dining table. I started walking down the stairs and Walt was waiting for me. One glance in his blue eyes, and the smile on his face was there. His said to me while I was coming down the staircase, "You are the most beautiful Queen I've ever seen, and your mine now and forever." He touched my hand, and I assured him "you are my beautiful King. I will love you forever." Everyone who was there at that moment just stared and said, "long live the King!" We walked towards the table all you could see was fruits laid out, eggs, boiled potatoes with herbs that smelled the whole room. They sat at the table and ate their meal. "My dear would you like to go for a stroll to the apple orchard on the mount, it's a beautiful day." The sun glared, and fresh chrysanthemum and cherry blossoms touched the windows as if cascading over it. "Yes, I love it." It is a great day for strolling through the fields. We laughed together, while he held my hand for a moment and walked to the beautiful fields of green. What a view it was, apple trees everywhere, flowers everywhere, and white roses too. As I walked through the fields my hand brushed through the beautiful flowers, "So beautiful." Margery said. I felt I was in heaven. He noticed how I loved flowers and said, "Margery, you know we can have it picked for you, and brought wherever you want them in the home." "Yes" I answered they are so beautiful. He glanced at me and said "Just like you" I blushed a little and he knew how to make me feel wonderful. Walt said to Margery, "I'll have the maids pick some apples so we can have apple pie tonight." "I think its splendid." We arrived in our quarters and Walt took me and his arms and embraced me. His soft had touched my skin as if fresh flower had touched my skin I felt a warmth, all through my body he smiled and said close your eyes, he said. "I have a surprise for you". I answered what kind of surprise? He said close your eyes and you'll understand so I closed my eyes, and I felt a cold around my neck he placed his hands and said now open your eyes. When I felt my neck there was a beautiful necklace around my neck with pearls. I said this is beautiful but why? You're my wife and I love you forever don't ever forget that. I answered, I will never forget that. I kissed his soft lips, and he embraced me so tight that I felt I was in heaven.

# Chapter 2
## The War

Jax ran down and told the King, "A war is coming." The next town is on fire. "We need all the men gathered and ready, to fight." All the bells rang, and the town was ready. The King said, "How many days, before they arrive?" "Two days." They said. We got ready, and I told Margery. She shed a tear. "Walt, do what you have to do for us, and for this town." He told her, "I will return to you, don't worry." I held his hand, and he held mine so tightly. We knew it wasn't easy. The day came, for battle. Horses ready, bells rang through the town. Men were on horses for battle. Jax said, "Sire, when your ready we charge" "let's charge now!" Our horses running through mud and blood. As we rode. Through swords on the floor, and bodies, that's all I saw. When it was over, we had won. We headed back, with our flag towards are kingdom. And put it back on its pole. "Glory to God."

He said. I ran in to see Margery. As I was running, she was running towards me. She started to cry, and he started to cry too. I was covered in blood, and mud. But she held me so tight. I said, "We won the battle!" "I love you, Margery. "I love you too." She answered. "Come get yourself changed and washed." said Margery. "I'll call the servants for dinner." Morning came and he whispered in my ear, "My dear, what plans do you have in mind for today?" Margery said, "I will be with my sisters, and I have a day planned together." "Great I will meet with my men and have a day with them." "Jax, Jax," yelled the king. "Yes, sire we can gather our men to go for a drink to celebrate our glory." The men headed to town. Had a few laughs at the tavern. It felt great. Margery took her sisters, to the apple orchard for the day. That evening they gathered for a beautiful meal. They cheered for their victory. The days that followed, they gathered the men to train outside for some training, just in case we need to battle again. We gathered our swords and headed to the grounds where our helpers' put things in place, for sword fighting and polls well attached to the grounds to fight and train. Jax called Michael, Jonah, Marcus. "Marcus call the rest of the men." "Yes, Jax and Jonah fix your hair, and call the men time for training men." They train hard with their swords all day in the heat until the King came out said, "Men it's time to come in, fine work. Come inside for refreshments and a good bath well do you men fine. Relax and enjoy the evening." Jax ran so fast for refreshments that he stumbled on a rock, and hit his knee, the pain he felt he yelled so loud that as if the birds were afraid to watch, the birds up above flew over his head so fast then everyone helped him up. The king said, "Jax come in, put some cold cloth on you knee and you'll be fine." "I know." he said, "Just that I was so thirsty and ran without looking." "I know Jax, the heat is too warm today, get some rest." That king had a rough voice that when he spoke you understand him. And you could remember his voice after it was spoken. The king had a heart of gold. He cared for his people and his family. That's why he was a man of strength and caring that was our King. The men carried Jax to his quarters and he rested for a while. While the others, prepared for dinner. Tonight, the king said to the cooks we will have chicken and potatoes and all the fixings for we shall dine with laughter and joy. Call upon the musicians to play for us we shall dance too. He came to our chambers, and he said, "Margery, wear that beautiful blue dress, of yours tonight and I shall wear a blue shirt to match." I looked at Walt he had that smile you just wanted to hug him so hard. And I smiled at him he saw my grin and he embrace me. How did he know what I was thinking, but he knew, come my dear let's get ready.

She called upon her ladies to braid her hair. She would usually leave her hair braided on both sides for every day, tonight she asked for them to braid her hair but pin it up with her crown on her head it will look splendid. She wore the pearl and diamond necklace Walt had given to her, she was ready for the evening the musicians played and my family was very happy. My mother, Madame Julia and her husband, captain Michael were dancing in the middle of the room, they were a nice pair. They were Married 50 years together. Laughing away in the room, came the girls all dressed up and smiling away. The men looked impeccable. The tables were all decked out with candle sticks and food for your eyes to see. Me and the King came in. Everyone was silent as we walked in. looking magnificent with our crowns on our head and grace. The King announced, let us feast tonight to my family and friends, everyone said "Long live the King." We sat at the middle of the table, and everyone looked at us, "we are a great couple." Walt said. The chicken smells delicious, the smell of lemon and herbs was wonderful. While we were eating, the girls Victoria, Alexandria, and Thea danced together it was grand, while Thea and Giacomo danced together. The other two girls were chosen by two men to dance with them. It was great, one was tall with blonde hair, the other real dark hair man with a great smile. They danced all night. My family decided to stay longer at court so we can spend some time together, I was very happy. The next morning, me and Walt decided to go horse riding, I loved the fresh air and so did he. The horses were ready, so we climbed on, and it was a little cold that day, but we decided to go anyway. We rode through the forest like we were the only two people there. I saw something in the grass I said to Walt. "I think it's a SNAKE!" At that moment, my horse decided to jump up and down. Walt got so scared, he yelled "Margery, hold tight." I tried but I fell off my horse. The moment I fell, I felt a pain on my back and just stared at the sky. There was fallen leaves underneath me, I just looked up and said, "Walt, I love you." he carried me on his horse. I can hear his heartbeat so fast when we arrived at the castle. All the attendants came to help, they carried me on my bed, and he called for the doctor to check me, and they put a cold cloth, and it was put on my back, and they put me to bed. Walt held my hand so tight and yelled, call the doctor now! They checked me and said I'll be fine in a few days. I whispered to his ear and said, "I'm a strong woman don't worry." He answered back and said, "I know, that's why you're my Queen." And a tear rolled down his cheek. He left my chambers and went down to have something warm to eat and asked the doctor to bring me hot blankets to keep me warm. I asked her ladies to give her some warm broth to drink. I drank my broth down slowly and when I finished, I fell asleep knowing I would be fine. Without me knowing Walt stayed by my side the whole night. The maids had told me the next morning. I woke up and felt a little better with the broth that I drank and having people to take care of me and Walt by my side helped me, my family came at a time to see me, to see how I'm doing. With the help and support, I said "I'll be on my feet very soon." My ladies came in and brushed my hair and took care of me. "Now, now" I said to my ladies. I'm not going to the ball, so stop fussing over me, and I smiled at them. "My lady we want you to look and feel well as soon as possible." The king is on his way to see you, have him come in I want to see him. He knocked at the door and said, "Margery, may I come in?" His blue eyes staring at me, I could just melt just with that, his smile was a joy to see. "Come in Walt", he kissed her forehead so softly and held my hand. "I miss you Margery, I want you to get better quickly, and I want for us to celebrate life." "Every moment is life." "I know", I answered him "I love you; I love you, now I'll leave you to the rest. I'll be back later to see how you are doing." He left and closed the door behind him. My smile was from one corner of my mouth to the other. He went to see his comrades and said, "Men let's get a few men to help with the moving of furniture around, so when

Margery gets on her feet she will be surprised and have a chest arriving just for her." "It's engraved with her name and mine and it can be passed down to our family." After a few days, Margery walked. They gave her a hot bath and wore a beautiful red gown. They put her hair up and she walked slowly to the reception area not knowing that Walt was hiding not so far from her. She looked around the room and was taken in. New linens of red on the tables and white candle sticks in the dining room. The bright light of candles shined through the dining room where me, and Walt dined that evening after the accident, life stood still for a moment. "Walt", she called out and I turned around and said, "So what do you think of this?" "I love this! It's wonderful!" she said. "I asked the men to help, and I asked the cooks to prepare your favorite meal, chicken and potatoes with fresh bread from the oven. This night was just for us." The cooks came in and curtsied. They left the food on the table. Walt said, "May I hold your hand?" And I said, "of course you're my king." He laughed because we would call each other King and Queen when we wanted to get something across. "How are you feeling tonight, Margery?" said the King. "I'm a lot better than I was a few days ago. Soon we can dance together again". Margery said. "I know" he said "I miss us together. I know in just a few more days, and all will be back too normal again." The King said.

The chicken melted in our mouths and the potatoes with fresh bread and herbs was delicious. "I love this meal" the King said. "Walt me too." Margery said. With a glass of wine, it was pleasant. "Come Margery I have a surprise just hold my hand and follow me to our chambers." They walked down the hall and everyone who was there said "Good evening my King and Queen" and they bowed. As we passed, we reached our quarters and he said, "Close your eyes and I closed my eyes, and he said now open them." When I opened my eyes a beautiful chest with our initials on it, M and W. I said to Walt "this is so beautiful and hugged him so tight it will be passed on to the next generation." The next morning the birds were chirping, and the sun came out in our room. We woke up. I saw her beautiful eyes and I smiled. I called the ladies I told them to give her some beautiful gowns and it would be laid out for her on our return. We will travel to the next town I want to show her around to everyone that you are a beautiful strong woman and my wife. They have all kinds of fresh bread laid out for us to choose and there's so much to see. The carriages came around and we got in. It was a warm and sunny day in the month of April springtime. My back was fine now, I kissed Walt, and he said to me today, "My Queen" and I laughed, we will do something special. While Walt, prepared something for her she didn't know that he had ordered beautiful fabric too. "The chest represents family, and it represents our future together." said Walt. Suddenly, we knew what this chest was all about. "Beautiful Walt" I said. "I love it." "I'm glad about everything you have been through this is a small token from me to you." With a kiss on my lips, he embraced me, and everything felt right now. "I know what life is, my King." Margery said, "I love you", my Queen." He answered. We retired for the night, and he blew the candle off the table, and he took me into his arms, and we fell asleep. I felt I was in heaven that's what I believe in my heart. I'm in heaven with Walt.

# Chapter 3
## A Trip to France

The next day we arrived to Honfleur France. The beautiful streets, people were happy to see us in their town. Our carriage stopped, a young child and her mother handed us some flowers I thanked them both. "My King, this is so sweet." "Yes, Margery now we shall be greeted at the castle just for us." We walked without guards in and its splendor. As we entered, it was magnificent. "Margery come they have prepared something for us to eat." The King said. We freshened up and decided to be greeted at this beautiful dining table with attendants to serve us while we ate. We were talking about having children of our own, once Margery is better from the accident. "Yes Walt, but for now let's enjoy the meal." We laughed together like children. We enjoyed each other's company. He understood me and I understood him. After lunch we walked to our chambers. While I was walking, my long coat touched the floor as I walked. I love the feeling of being happy with myself and how I felt walking down the corridor. The attendants said "Sire, you may go into town, where there is a beautiful shop where your Queen can look at jewelry and you can choose something for her." The servant said. "Yes, my King. We shall go. The fresh air, will do us good." Margery said. We both got into the carriage, and we rode with Margery's green eyes looking at everywhere we went. I was so happy looking at her face as we rode through the streets. The wind blowing through her blond hair made me smile. She was the love of my life. "Hey Margery, whatever you like it's yours." "I will choose something, but I have everything that I need Walt and that's you." Margery said. He smiled and made it her day. She saw a beautiful brooch. "It will look splendid." The Queen said. They gave it to us in a pretty cloth, wrapped in blue. We rode past the bread shop the smell was everywhere, and me and Walt looked at each other. That will hit the spot. "I know Margery, we will pick one up." My guard put it in the carriage then we passed by the forest which was so beautiful in the spring, flowers blooming, and the fresh smell of grass. Margery loved that and so did I. We returned to the castle, where the servants saw the bread and placed it before us so that we may have it tonight. They prepared a basin full of hot water with jasmine in it and Margery soaked in it as I saw her, I said you are beautiful her hair was up with pins and her body was beautiful. I said to Margery, "I want to spend time for us." "Yes, Walt, I miss you dearly." He bathed too and I looked at him, you are beautiful you know. That's why I love you. He smiled put his hands on the basin and got up, water splashing everywhere and walked towards me. He kissed me so deeply and I felt his touch and we went on the bed, and we made love. He said in my ear, "you are mine always." "Yes" Walt replied to Margery. We covered ourselves with the bed linens and fell asleep in each other arms. The next morning, we woke up and were hungry because we forgot to eat last night so this morning the servants warmed up the bread with butter and fruits, and eggs and knocked at our door. "Yes, my lord, food is ready we shall be down in a few moments. Thank you." Walt grabbed my arm and kissed my hand. "My love last night was wonderful." "I know, I've missed us since the accident." "Well now things will be as they should, do you agree?" "Yes, Walt kissing you is my happiness and loving you is my heaven." "Me too Margery. Now let's go eat before we shall starve." They walked towards the dining area the smell of that fresh bread and cheese and fresh baked pie made us sigh with delight smiled at each other like children, we started to eat. "Isn't it splendid how wonderful to have this abundance of foods." "Yes, my lady we have what we need." said the cooks, and they curtsied and left. "It's been fabulous spending the quiet time together Walt. But we soon must go back, I have scheduled a few things to take care of." said The Queen. "When we're ready, we shall travel back home." Said The Queen. Later that afternoon, flowers were sent to our room and the whole room had a beautiful fragrance to it. Margery looked at the flowers and smiled, "My Walt, this is beautiful I hope you like it." He knew she did, because she loved flowers. She smelled them as if taking a huge breath of air, "wonderful" she said. "Walt If we can walk in the garden, it would be wonderful." He put on his coat, and she did as well. It was still kind of cool in April, but the smell of fresh flowers blooming and the fountains flowing with water made it a great afternoon. We smiled and Walt took me by my waist. He touched my cheeks "it's cold" The Queen said. "I know" he said. And we both smiled. His eyes made me know that he loved that fresh air and walking just like me. We marched and headed home; on our way we passed trees with flowers blooming it was beautiful. The horses came to a stop, we reached our castle, and our attendants were waiting for us to dismount the carriage. I got out first and they greeted us, "Welcome home my Queen." Next was Walt to come out. "Welcome home my King." Pleasant trip Sire, "yes very pleasant". I couldn't wait to see my family at court and everyone, Julia came running saying my daughter you look fabulous. "You glow." "Thank you, mother." "It was a pleasant trip have you noticed anything else?" she said "yes, the beautiful brooch on your coat." "Yes, Walt bought it for me." "It's beautiful." Thank you, mother. She greeted Walt and me and my mother walked down the corridor. The king walked down the corridor and stopped at the kitchen to tell the cook to prepare something delicious for the home coming tonight, we shall celebrate our return home for me and Margery. The cooks said "We will have her favorite meal and we'll bake apple pies," The king replied, "Yes. That's splendid". Dinner time came and everyone gathered at the banquet. Me and Margery dressed up for dinner, but tonight we wore red. Margery wore a beautiful red gown that was laid out for her. "It was a surprise from me." The King said. While we were away, a collection of gowns were done for Margery. She put her hand on her mouth and said, "Walt but how?" The dress was beautiful, with pearls around the neck and small pearls to pin her hair up." He grinned and said as always, "A small token." He would do things like this and then smile. I grabbed his arm and kissed him. Margery said, "I don't know what to say." "Say nothing." He spoke. Your other gowns are on our chest. We wrapped it for you to see later. Come now we must go to dinner everyone is waiting. When they came too, the banquet hall, everyone looked at them both. Wow, all their mouths stayed open with amazement. We took our place, and the King made a toast to his wife, and he said, "My Queen you are my beauty and my courage I thank you." "This feast is for her and for everyone here. Hold your cups high." Everyone said, "To the Queen." She kind of blushed and smiled, the food started coming out of the kitchen she knew the aroma baked chicken roasted potatoes and vegetables and of course apple pie. She whispered in Walt's ear. "I love you.", and he smiled he puts his hand on top of hers and she knew his answer. The gesture came tonight to resight poems, everyone enjoyed it. When dinner was done Margery and Walt went to their chambers to retire for the night. She told Walt, "I'll look at the gowns tomorrow. I'm a little tired from the trip and all, why yes, come I'll untie your dress." His soft hands loosened the back of my dress and it fell to the ground. He embraced me and touched me, he undressed himself and got in bed with me, the passion between is always there. He kissed my lips softly and touched my skin so softly. We made love. That night, we could see the moon light out. We fell asleep in each other's arms. Morning came, and I had my maid pour me a hot bath. While Walt decided to take his in his other room. He had meetings to take care of his said. "Margery, don't forget late afternoon we'll meet in the throne room." Walt was going to surprise her with a new task being Queen. I'll be there, while the basin was filling up, she rose from her bed and slowly went in, felt so good the warm water and a feeling of peace came over her. The view from her window was beautiful, lush green hills and flowers overlooking the grounds. Once she came out of the bath, she dressed in blue to meet Walt in the throne room. He smiled by far and I came towards him with the smile. He said, "Margery, I want you to take notes on meetings and events. This way, we both know what's happening about the castle and its people". I was delighted. "Yes, it's great. I can sit beside you and learn." "Now, we can have breakfast and we'll talk about what are schedule is like for today." Walt said. Margery looked at Walt and said, "Yes we can start with breakfast" she said. The lieutenant Jax, walked in the room and passed towards them, "I'm sorry to intrude sire, but our troop wants to know what we shall do for today." "Now you see Margery, this is what it's like to be me." Walt said. "Now Lieutenant Jax. Margery will also be listening, and you will be taking orders from her to inform the troops." "This is what it is all about." Walt said. "Yes, Sire." And he left. Me and Margery ate our breakfast, and she came with a suggestion. "Why don't the men arrange the ball room." Margery said. "Walt, I have a few ideas. My birthday is coming up and I was thinking we shall have a ball." "I think that's a great idea! Margery." Walt said. "I will inform Jax, and they will come to you on what you need done."

"I will go look at the stables to see if everything is fine with the horses." Walt said. The King called Jax to take care of the Queen's orders and I went to look at the horses. As I'm walking in, I see my horses looking at me as if to say, "hey we miss you, soon we'll go for a ride." I looked at my horses it's been busy, I called the attendants to water down the horses and clean their area. All was well, I took a fresh breath of air outside of the stables felt refreshed and ready for the afternoon. Jax arrived at the ballroom, and Margery started to call him for what to do for the grand ball. "Jax, I want everything in red, white, and gold and lots of food and music, I want to send invitations to everyone at court it will be a masquerade ball. Everyone must wear a mask." The Queen said. "Yes, My Queen" answered Jax. Jax left and went to speak to Lieutenant Michael, Marcus, and Jonah. "Men the Queen asked us to get the ball room in order because a ball will take place. Let's get all the help. She wants white, red, gold, candles everywhere, food and music, we will need to get, tables all in a row and one in front for the King and Queen. We need the gesture to sing and play music and we need to get the place all lavished for the ball. Candle stick, chandeliers cleaned, linens, curtain's cleaned, curtains changed, let's get it all together!" "We shall tell the King preparations are on its way. What food shall the cooks get for that night?" "This time I think duck shall be great for the menu." said the King. Duck, potatoes and greens, and for dessert baked cake with apples, on the side dish cheese, and bread and fruits, it will be grand. The King was so proud of Margery for taking things in her own hands. She is doing a great job. The invitations were sent out, and the ball room was looking grand with candles of white, linens and everything was coming together. I decided to go speak with Margery I approached our bedroom, and she was combing her long blond hair. She knew he was there because of his walk into the room. The King embraced her and said, "I love when you brush your hair it's like silk, you are beautiful, and you make me proud on giving orders to the men and knowing what to do if ever I am ill." "Don't say that, Walt." Margery said. "Of you being ill." "I know." He said. "But we must look at things in a different matter just in case." She took her hand and touched his strong and beautiful face; you are my strength and my world. And that's why I love you. He turned around and said, that's why I love you. "Have you looked at your gowns?" the King said. She replied "There's one. Just beautiful for the ball." "I know." she said. "You love the colors red and blue. Let me know which one, so we can match at court." "Yes Walt, our masks are coming soon for us and the whole court." Margery said. "Great Margery. Would you like to go for a stroll around the grounds this afternoon?" Walt said. "Why yes, Walt. Fresh air and a good walk, will be great." Margery said. "I know I feel the same way as you." Walt said. We decided to go for a stroll. We went through the big iron doors and walked out with the sun shining and the grounds were so pretty. "The fresh air, feels great doesn't it, Margery?" "Yes, it does" she said. We walked all around the grounds and spend a lovely evening and talked together. At that moment I felt a bit dizzy. He held my hand and said, "maybe you should rest with all the event we did today." "Maybe it was too much." Walt said. She agreed and went to lie down on her bed. "If you don't feel up to it Margery for supper will bring the food here for you." Walt said. "Yes Walt, that sounds better for tonight." Margery said. Walt addressed the cooks to bring supper in our chamber for tonight. I prepared soft candles, wine and a great dinner. We had dinner that night. She looked so beautiful that night, that she was glowing. Later that night, we fell asleep together. The next morning, she got up. I held her hand, and said, "Are you alright Margery?" Walt said. "I'll call the doctor if you're not feeling well." The doctor was called in. He came in, and said, "I'll wait outside." Walt said. Once he checked her, he said to her, "You're pregnant! I need you to not to do any stressful activities." The doctor said. I was so surprised and so happy at the same time. The doctor left and smiled at the King. Walt walked in and she had a big smile across her face. "What is it, Margery?" Walt said. "Walt" she held his hand "we are expecting a child Walt". He jumped with happiness and kissed Margery. "This is the most beautiful news my darling. When shall we tell everyone?" "We will them at the ball Walt." She said. "I can't wait for this child to be born and to tell the news to everyone. They will be very happy for us." "I'll leave you to rest and I shall have some wine for my happy news. I'll come back later so we can have dinner tonight at the dining room" the King said. "Yes, Walt I think it's excellent." She said. The ladies came in to see if I'm okay. Alexandria, Thea and Victoria. "Are you well my Queen?" Victoria said. "Yes, I'll be fine." she said. She didn't want to tell anyone yet. I just need to get dressed up so I can walk a little and get ready for dinner. "Come girls let's have a few laughs. Let's get some cake downstairs and let's not tell the cooks they're going to be upset who stoled the food." said Alexandria. "Then we'll tell them later." said Thea. "Get me anything that has cream on it." said the Queen. The girls laughed and said "She is in a good mood today." said Thea. The girls ran downstairs and took what they could and laughed "Come Victoria."

said Thea. "Get that one too!" we were laughing but trying to keep it quiet at the same time. They couldn't hold it in and laughed. They ran back to the Queen's chambers and closed the door. The Queen was laughing too, "You girls." she said. "Let's sit on my bed and don't tell anyone that were eating like this." The Queen said. They shared the food and laughed and wondered what the cooks are thinking right now. Everyone had cream on their lips and faces what a laugh we had. "But now girls it's time to get ready." The Queen said. "Yes, My Queen" they said. They got her dressed up and got her hair done and dressed her. Then she left her quarters with the ladies behind her. "Girls let me tell the cooks," said the Queen. She went in the kitchen. The cooks were in panic. "Who took the sweets!" The Queen said. "We don't know who came in and took the sweets Madame." said the cook. The Queen replied, "It's me and my ladies, we were hungry for sweets." "It's alright your Majesty we will make more of it." said the Cook. The Queen left with a grin on her face. She felt like a kid and went to the dining room. Walt was standing in the dining room and stopped and looked at his Queen coming in. He bowed at her, and said, "May I have this dance?" She smiled and said, "why yes, My King." They danced with no music on just them two. Just them looking at each other and knowing that she was carrying his child. They finished dancing and they sat down for a romantic dinner. Candles were lit, and food was marvelous, especially with those potatoes with butter and herbs. We ate and then walked hand in hand towards the grounds. "My dear, the ball preparation are in order." The King said. "Yes, my King. Thank you." The Queen said. "That's great, and how's my wife tonight carry our baby." The King said. "I'm fine." She replied. She looked at his bright eyes that shined. He said, "I am the luckiest man alive." "We shall announce the news at the ball." The Queen said. "I think we shall wear red." The King said. Her red gown with black trim and a red mask will look great. And Walt wearing a red suit and a black jacket with the same mask. "That's splendid! Now let's go for a walk before we go to bed." Said the King. We strolled through the grounds. "Look Walt! Look how many stars are out tonight." "Look a fallen star make a wish." she said. He closed his eyes and made a wish. The wind was blowing lightly, and it was beautiful. We stopped near a beautiful tree of chrysanthemum and Walt took me in his arms and kissed me. "I love this, this to me is a beautiful night under the stars." Margery said. "Beauty is everywhere." I said to Walt. He knew I loved walks, moonlight walks, and the smell of beautiful flowers. "You are so beautiful to me Margery the way you hold yourself and the way you talk, it's like you see things differently than someone else." Walt said. "I just see beauty everywhere I go.

I'm starting to understand it myself, because of you." Walt said. We walked towards our chambers, and we kissed each other goodnight. Morning came and we saw how bright the sun was shining. "Another beautiful day Walt." Margery said. "I will get the crew out today we will practice arrow shooting, and sword mastering so if ever we had to go battle, we're ready." Walt said. "I will check court if there's anything happening in town we should know about." Walt said. A peasant was waiting for me, for an answer on stock. I would answer him to tell him what to do. His cow was found dead, and he didn't know why. I asked, "Was it time for it to die or was it sick?" The peasant replied, "Sire, she was fine yesterday, she died of old age What do you suggest sire?" He said. "Cut it up and eat it quickly" The King said. "Don't let it linger for diseases." The Queen said. "Thank you, my Queen it shall be done." The peasant said. The man left court happy. The king was happy about what Margery did. He said to himself "That's my Queen." She knows how to handle anything. I'm proud of her, and I'll tell her tonight. He walked down the hall and at the end of the chambers he entered the room where Margery was. "I heard what you did and I'm so proud of you, you truly are my other half." She smiled and said, "I love doing this and helping people at court." They would look at us, not because we were King and Queen but just the way we took care of our people and their needs.

# Chapter 4
## Masquerade Ball

That same night. We headed to our chambers, and we got ready for the ball. I had put my red dress on with pearls around my neck with that ruby clasp and red feather in my hair. Walt had a red shirt with the matching mask. We looked great. Music was coming from the ball room. As we were walking towards the ballroom, with my long train. The doors opened. Where people were all gathered with their masks, and it was all lit with candles. It was spectacular. We walked in and everyone gasped how beautiful we looked. We took our dance on the floor and at that moment all the eyes were on us. Yes, we were King and Queen, but we were just like everybody else. I looked at him with amazement and he looked at me the same way. When the music stopped everyone clapped, the king asked for everyone to be seated. "I have an announcement to make." said The King. He took his cup and raised it up. "My wife and I are expecting our first child, may we celebrate this evening with joy and good days ahead." Everyone said to the King and Queen "Congratulations". They repeated it twice to the "King and Queen". The dinner arrived at the table we had seven courses that night. We had duck, potatoes, greens, cakes, everything you could imagine was here tonight at court. Music was playing people danced and the girls danced with the two men, who asked them to dance. Victoria danced with Comte Brice. He said, "You look so beautiful in that blue dress." Victoria smiled back at him and said, "Thank you Comte Brice." They walked on the terrace, and he held her hand. And they kissed. Alexandria danced with Comte Richard. After the dance they went and sat near a beautiful window with glace painting on it and they had some wine and danced all night. The men liked the women so much that they asked them at court if they wanted to court them and they agreed. Then Thea and Comte Giacomo were very happy for the girls. The wine kept pouring and the King danced with his Queen. He looked in her eyes and he smiled and said sweetheart in her ear "I love you." He got close to her soft lips and kissed her. You light up the room with your smile. You are the perfect wife, my love, my joy. They danced and everyone smiled at them. They were so beautiful together, than the King stopped the music and said "everyone" look at the doors. We all looked and waited. A beautiful cake arrived "all lit up" with the initials M&W on the cake. The room was all lit like a night sky with stars everywhere. This is a surprise for my "Queen". Everyone said "to the Queen" the cooks took the cake in the other room to have it cut. While Margery looked at Walt & said, "to my husband". They raised a glass, and everyone said, "To the Queen." Let's all rejoice. The music kept on playing. All were dancing, laughing & the evening was wonderful. One lieutenant was eating cake, how drunk he was he had it all over himself and his wife kissed his face and said "darling we can share it together" everyone laughed. The King laughed so hard and said, "I'm sure you can share it together." Everyone at court laughed. The night ended, and everyone retired. They all said, "goodnight my King and Queen." The king said have a good night, everyone. The evening ended. Walt took Margery's hand and kissed it and told the gesture to play a beautiful melody. We danced together, and Walt said, "my dear it was a great evening and it's all because of you." I said, "no it's because of us." He said "yes, we are one mind and one heart that's for sure." "May our children be blessed with what we have, and compassion and love. It is the utmost important in life." We danced and once the music was done, we left the ballroom to go to our chambers. It was a beautiful evening, but I was a little tired and Walt understood. We feel asleep so quickly that night. I think people will be talking about this for a long time to come. "Walt, tell the servants, I want flowers in my room and I want the servants to draw me a hot bath and then we shall get the day started." The king asked the servants to do as Margery asked and the hot bath was done, and they went picking flowers for her. "I will tell Jax, to handle the men today, and make them train outside it's a beautiful day. I want to take you for a walk where I first met you on my horse." said Walt. We will pass by the pond, and we'll see the trees and flowers and talk. "I think it's great Walt, let's do that." We both got dressed for the day. I loved when he brushed his hair and he looked beautiful, it's like I'm in a cloud when I look at him. He makes my heart jump. I feel that sense of when someone is so close that you can't breathe but you can. We walked down the corridor, and everyone looked at us, and said, "Good morning your majesties." "Good morning" answered the King. "We shall be near the grounds for a walk, if you need me, I shall be with The Queen." said The King. "Please tell the cooks to prepare something for us when we get back." He told

Jax to tell the cooks. "Yes Sire." Jax left went to tell the cooks and went towards his comrades. "Hey man, today the King gave me orders to train outside and we shall, it's a beautiful day" "Alright men let's go!" "Hey Jonah, Marcus, a word" The two men came close to Jax "what is it?" "The woman that we met wants us to escort them again tonight, I think it's great." "They're very pretty and I think we shouldn't disappoint them." "Send this message to them, for tonight we shall meet them." "I'll send word," said Marcus. When we got back, they prepared us trout, and they also had pasta. The woman received the news and got ready for the evening. Night came and the men got ready well-groomed and walked out of the castle gates. "Hey, Marcus would you want her for your wife?" "The blonde girl her name is Isabella." Jax said. "Yes, if she agrees. What about you Jonah?" "The same as you, we will see what happens tonight at the tavern." The men met the women just before the door to the tavern halls. The ladies said to Jax, "Hello everyone let's get inside." Jax held the door and opened it for the ladies, as they walked in the tavern. They got a table and ordered ale for everyone. "Ladies what's new?" Marcus asked. One answered well at court "the Queen is expecting, we're so happy for her and the ball was so beautiful." "Yes" Jax said, "us men helped organize it with the Queen." The drinks came and they started talking and drinking.

The laughter was loud at the tavern. "All is well Jonah." said to the person who left the drinks down. "Yes, thank you." Jonah asked Emma to go for a walk outside and they went out of the tavern. "Emma." Jonah said. "We've talked for a while; I'd like to know if you want to court me. I really do like you." Emma said "same thing." Jonah was so happy that he kissed her on her cheek. They went back to the tavern and sat happy together. Jax and Marcus asked the women the same thing and all were happy because it seemed everyone liked each other. The night was getting late, so they left a tip to the man, and they all left together outside of the tavern. They all walked hand in hand as they reached the castle gates. The women went in, and the men followed, now ladies don't forget tomorrow we will go for a walk on the grounds together. Yes, they replied. Jax went in giggling. The men turned around and said "merci" to the women, that means, "thank you in English." Jax turned to the men and said, "hey man I think we're all courting these women." "Aren't we lucky men." Jax said. "Three guys and three beautiful women." "Right men." "Yes Jax" Jonah answered. The King greeted the men and said, "hey man, you seem so happy tonight, why yes, your highness we have found our wives." "Well, well man, I'm happy for you." said The King. "Now, how was the training?" "Well sire everything went alright. So, I'll see you in the morning." "Yes Sire." said the men. The King went into the chambers. Margery looked beautiful, her long blonde hair around her waist and she was brushing her hair. "My darling you look wonderful" and he kissed her soft cheek. She looked at him with her green eyes and said, "come onto the bed." He left his sword on the side of the bed and starting undressing, he looked at his wife with love, what they have is something out of this world. You could tell by the way they look at each other and smile for no reason. She embraced her King, and they made love that night. Next morning, the sun was so bright with the birds chirping they woke up. "Hello, my Queen," said The King. She said, "hello my King." They smiled at each other, and he looked into her eyes and just smiled. She said, "why you look at me this way?" He said, "I love looking at you, you're beautiful." She kissed his lips, and they got up to start their day. She put on her green gown on, and her hair was brushed so nice and braided and she told Walt "Let's get breakfast to eat." We entered the dining hall all was set on the table ready for us to eat. Our chairs were pulled, and we sat down. The smell of fresh bread was wonderful so fresh. We ate cheese, fruits and it was wonderful. "Walt, I want to tell you I would like to go for a walk on the grounds." "Yes" he said. And he kissed my forehead. He took my hand, and we started on our walk near the fountain.

After our walk, Walt marched to see the men. He walked in and saw Michael "send Jax to me." The king said. "Let's get the men to do their daily exercises on the grounds and then we will feast at supper time." "Yes Sire." The king put his regular clothes to go on the grounds and the men followed. The sun was so bright outside, but we started on one-on-one fighting with our swords. Then we started running around the grounds a few times all around so we can keep in shape. We gathered all around. We drank some ale, and we walked inside, thank God it was fresh in the castle.

# Chapter 5
## A New Beginning

The king went to see Margery and she looked at him with her green eyes and she looked at him with his blue eyes. "Tell the maids to prepare the basin for my bath." The maids came in and the water was prepared. Margery prepared herself for the afternoon, and the king dressed himself with the pretty blue shirt, and he was ready for the day. Margery walked with him, hand in hand down the hallway. She smiled, "do you see anything different?" he looked at her and noticed her bump and bowed to her. And smiled. Her train was so beautiful light green all the way to the floor while she walked. She looked beautiful. They walked to the dining room and Margery said to Walt. "I think I will change the draperies in the dining room, I want them all in blue and white." "Anything you want darling." The king said. "Now let's get breakfast and see what our schedule today will be." They went to the palace room for discussions, where they sat on a table with papers to discuss the coming events. They decided to walk together at the palace meeting room to write a book on what it entails to keep the palace tidy in his kingdom. "Everything needs to be put on paper. Stock, how many people live here and so forth." Margery was so happy. The meeting went on for about two hours. Then they decided to have lunch together. Commander Jax sent word to the rest of the troops that once the King would finish his supper, a meeting would take place. Jax sent word to the men, that once we finish supper that the whole dining room needed changing and that the nursery for the baby would need to be in place in the Quarters. In a few months, the baby is due on August 12. The room needs taken care of. Jax sent word and the project was in hand. "Merci Jax." said The King. "Yes Sire." He walked out and called his commanders, and everything was in process. Night fall came and Jax sent word to his superior that the preparations was on their way. The curtains were changed It was to be impeccable for the arrival of the baby. Margery walked out onto the terrace and touched her stomach knowing a King would be born soon. Walt followed her and said, "this will be the beginning of history for us." The sun was setting, and you could see past the grounds and onto the open fields. Flowers were everywhere and fountains and our palace was grand. It wasn't important the number of homes we had, it was the people and our kingdom that matter the most. Walt took my hand and looked at my eyes and I looked at his, we didn't need to say anything. We loved each other and it was a love like no other. We walked hand in hand inside and the fresh breeze felt great. "Margery let's get the servants to prepare something for tonight." "I think fresh fruits and a great broth would do fine." said The King. Margery answered, "yes that sounds great for tonight." They walked in the dining hall, the food arrived. The white plates and the gold goblet with ruby stones looked beautifully. Now, Walt said to Margery "let's sit and eat this splendid meal." The broth was great the smell of it took over the entire room. The next day we had a message that arrived and when a message arrives it's either good news or bad. I was summoned to the grand hall the messenger came into the grand gates. "Your highness a message has arrived." Before opening it, Walt touched the envelope with his hand. He sat on his throne and read it. "My brother if you are reading this I have passed on. I've loved you since we were children, and I shall love you forever. My lands I leave with you and my wife shall remain at your hands. And my other homes, belongs to my sons. Take care my brother we'll see each other in another lifetime." I took the letter and embraced it to my chest. I stood still for a moment and started to cry. I knew going down to Avignon and Rouen would take days. I announced it to the kingdom that, a day of mourning would take place. Me and my wife took the day to pray at the cathedral. The end of the day the men came around to pay their respect to the King. Michael, Jax, Marcus, Jonah and the rest of the troops. May this day be a day not to be forgotten. It was May 25, my brother is now in heaven. "Men take this moment of silence." said the King. All the men bowed their heads. "Thank you, men, now we'll feast for the night." Everything was prepared and set in the dining hall. Everything was brought out. We dined and ate until it was twelve o'clock and we told the priest to ring the church bells at midnight. Everyone stopped eating and bowed with their heads to his brother. "May he see heaven and be at peace." The king stood up with his goblet and said "to my brother up in heaven. Peace be with you now and forever. Until we meet again" some people at court started crying. It was a time to remember our loved ones. Then we resumed our meal. Everyone said we will welcome your brother's wife with open arms. And me and Margery were the last to leave the dining hall. We walked into the quarters and me and Margery were so tired as soon as we got to bed, we fell asleep. Morning came and Margery was now about seven months pregnant. Baby is due in September. The carriages arrived. My brother's wife and her belongings. The bell was rung, and the servants gathered at the gate. I stood there to greet my sister-in-law, Colette. With Margery and my attendants. She came out of the carriage. She has long black hair, and pretty face that I still remember when I used to visit. "Hello Colette." Margery said. I'm so sorry for your loss. Colette hugged Margery and said "Yes, thank you." "He was ill at the end of his life." Walt embraced her too and said Colette welcome to your home. Follow us we'll show you to your quarters. The maids will be coming in if you need anything or a hot bath. "We'll leave you alone but we all dine at seven at night in the dining hall." We left Colette alone and me and Margery walked to our quarters. Got changed and ready for the evening. All kinds of food was prepared, and the dining hall was ready for the evening. Colette came in with a dark colored dress and sat next to Margery. I rose off my seat and made a speech. "This evening is dedicated to my brother, raise your glass. To my brother who I loved so much, may you rest in peace, and may God give you everything you need." Everyone said, "here here." We finished our supper and headed to our chambers. We sat in our quarters and discussed about Colette. "I think she should be fine here, what do you think Margery?" "Yes Walt."

said Margery. "Where would she go?" the King said. "We will make her feel at home and have her do activities, so she won't think too much about my brother. I know how hard it must be on her. We will make her do things to keep her mind off." "Come my darling, I'll help you undress with your baby bump. You have a hard time to undress." He unsnapped her dress and the dress fell to the ground. He helped her with her under garments and said, "Margery, my darling. You are so beautiful." and kissed her neck. He took her in his arms and kissed her again, and whispered in her ear. I love you come, and we made love that night just by looking at each other we understand each other. Morning came, the basin was filled with water and fresh flowers, and I put myself slowly in it. It felt great. Walt got ready for the day and kissed my forehead. "I will see you later sweetheart." He closed the door and left. I relaxed in the warm water and the maids combed my hair. "My Queen are you ready to come out?" the maid said. "Yes, I am." Margey said. They put a towel and wrapped me. I decided to put a blue gown today. "My ladies can you help me with my dress?" "Yes, your highness." They said. They helped me with a blue gown and put my nice pearl necklace on. I went to Colette's quarters. "Hi Colette, how are you today?" Margery said. "I'm fine." Colette answered. "I love that gown you are wearing Margery." "Thank you, come with me I'll show you around the castle, and later we can go for a nice walk on the grounds." Breakfast is ready. Let's get to the dining area. "Do you smell the fresh bread?" Margery said. "Yes, I do." said Colette. We sat at the table and the cooks brought out some fresh fruits and fresh bread, tarts. Colette and I ate. "What was it like, when you gave birth to your children" she said. "I was fine afterwards it's going to be fine Margery." She held my hand and said, "thank you." "I know the circumstances aren't great but I'm glad you're here for this child to be born." We looked at each other and smiled. Now let's go for that walk. They went out in the Terrance and took a walk in the garden. Then she saw Walt, and told Colette, "Have a great evening I need to have a word with Walt." That evening she wasn't feeling well. She grabbed Walt's arm, and said, "The baby is coming." They changed her and brought her to the labor room. The Labor women were ready. In my head, she said, "Thank god the nursey is ready." The labor women told me to push. With all my might I started pushing. She pushed, and pushed. And the baby was here. Walt came running hearing a baby cry. "My child is born" the King said. They took Margery to the bedroom, with fresh linens and covered her, and made her hold her baby. "It's a boy." The King came in and said, "It's a boy!" "Ring the tower bells." He said. "A new King has been born!"

the King said. "He held his son, for the first time, and started to cry." He kissed Margery on her forehead and said, "You have made me proud." "We shall name him, Willam."

# Chapter 6
## A Festival

Two months passed, and Walt said, "Tomorrow it's a big day for William and for us. All the court and beyond will know of it." The King said. "Yes, they will,". Margery said. We headed to our chambers because tomorrow is going to be a long day. Morning came, and the carriages came to the gates. All in a row, with white horses, all groomed. We were all greeted at the gates. We got into the carriages and went to the cathedral, where the whole town knew what was going on. There were shouting on the streets. "Long live the King." We arrived at the Cathedral. As we entered, everyone took their seats. The ceremony was almost complete. They put water over his head, and he was baptized. I never felt so happy like this. Now we were headed for the feast to take place at the castle. We arrived, and the smell of everything cooking was great. We entered the ballroom, and everyone was there. All the men, in their sharp suits, and the women in their elegant gowns. As we entered the ballroom with beautiful glass doors. Everyone clapped. The King and I took our seats on the throne. The king made a speech. He held his cup high. "My son, my future Heir, and to the future King." "May tonight be a beautiful celebration." Everyone took their seats and started eating. The music was playing, and the people were dancing. We laughed and danced all night. The celebration ended, and we headed back to our chambers. Me and Walt were very tired and went to bed. The next morning, we asked the maids to clean the ballroom. Me and Walt will be heading for Paris to see what is happening there, and what we should do for our people. We will be leaving the day after tomorrow. Let the staff know. They curtsied and left the room. Jack was summoned to take care of the men, while I'm away and the adviser was to take care of the palace. We prepared our chest to be transported onto the carriages. Our men were getting ready to voyage. The next morning, we left, his brother had left us his lands. So, we went and see what it entailed. We arrived at the gates, and there were beautiful trees of apples, and flowers. "Just as I remembered." said Walt. The town is called Rouen. We walked in and the attendants greeted us at the gates. We entered and they brought us to our quarters to rest. Our baggage's were brought in. We were in a beautiful room, all red and white. "Isn't it beautiful Walt?" he replied "Yes, it is." We changed and sat at the grand hall to see what to do, with the palace and everything else. Me and Margery took a book and started to write. Three homes were ours, and we had told ourselves it will belong to our children. We had the cooks cook something for us. We sat at the ground hall. They brought us geese on a bed of herbs and potatoes. We sat on the highchairs. Not the throne chairs, they were for my brother and his wife. We enjoyed our meal with a nice glass of wine. We should walk around the grounds later to look at everything. I felt at home. We strolled room to room, until we got to the grounds, and walked outside. The sun was shining, and it was a very nice day. Margery asked. If fresh flowers will be brought to the chambers. The maids were sent to prepare some flowers to be sent to their chambers. It was a beautiful breeze outside. He held her hand and said, "I love you, my Queen." She looked at Walt and said, "You are my love, and my King." The sun was shining like a picture-perfect scenery. "Margery, will you walk with me to my brother's chambers?" "I need you beside me. I can't walk there alone." "I'm here for you." said Margery. And so, they held hands and walked to his brother's chambers. Everything was left intact. His sword was laid out near his bed. Shining and polished with ruby rhinestones. His clothes were still there, and I could picture him wearing this. she said to Walt. "Your brother will not be forgotten; he was a good man. I want to bring back home his sword. And keep it with us." "We'll keep it were everyone can see it." He said. He wanted to cry, and Margery kissed his cheek. He knew what it meant. "I'm alright." said the King. Later that knight, we had supper. We were served chicken with lemon and herbs. We sat down and they held our chairs before sitting. We drank our wine, and the food was delicious. We finished our meal, and we headed to our chambers. We were tired, from the whole voyage. The next day, we went to visit the scenery for fresh air, and Margery picked up a necklace on her way. A beautiful necklace to go with her green eyes. It was wrapped and ready for her. We road to the streets, and it felt wonderful. Then we saw a poor man on the street with torn clothes, I had them stop the carriage. I called the man. He turned around, I told my attendant to give him some coins. The men said, "Sire, I'm grateful for this." "May I know your majesty's name?" I answered "King Walt." "I will never forget this." The peasant said. "Thank you Sire." They got back to the castle and got their things in order. For they had to go back home. Everything is done, and we decided to get ready for our journey home. The carriages were ready, and we parted. I took my brothers sword and wrapped it up and brought it with us. We road through the night and arrived back at our castle. The adviser and the main people at court were right infront of our gates. They all bowed when we stepped out of the carriage. I told Michael to bring the sword to the red room, so that we can put up his sword. Colette came to the room running and bowed. "My husband sword has been brought." "Yes Colette, everything is in order at your home." "We gave the attendance money so they can stay for a while." "The other two homes, we took over." "We had a good trip." "I miss him though." She put her hand out, and he held her hand. Collette said, "I miss him too, he was my husband." "I'll go see Margery." She said. She walked out of the red room and saw Margery in the hall. "Hi, my darling." Colette kissed Margery. "I heard the trip went well." "Thank you, and Your home was beautiful." said Margery. "I heard Jax, and the two men are getting married, we shall prepare for the wedding."

# Chapter 7
## Three Weddings

The following day, the three men went to their rehearsal all together. The women got everything ready, and the men went to get gifts for their wife's to be. The dresses were ready. And the day has come. The carriages were ready at the gates, for the day. We arrived at the cathedral and the people were waiting outside. The people were all clapping, the men were all dressed up. Then at 1:00 the ceremony started. It was beautiful. We danced, and the music was playing. Jax spoke into the king's ear, "Sire, thank you for doing this for us." "We are forever grateful." The king whispered in his ear, and said, "My men you mean everything to me." Jax smiled and returned to their celebration. Me and Margery danced, it was a beautiful night. After the celebration the men and women retired for the night. Some were a little drunk, and who was laughing hysterically. It was a happy night. Fast forward in time me and Margery had six more children. We had seven in total, Willam, Cecilia, Robert, Richard, Margaret, Sofia and Matilda. They were healthy and happy as any family can be. They would come all over the castle running and laughing, it was a great time. The ladies decided to get married as well. Victoria had beautiful black hair. And she and her Comte Brice got married. Alexandria and Comte Robert got married one month later. Everyone at court was happy for them. The days that followed were great. My little one sat on my lap and looked and me and smiled. She was 9 months old, she had blue eyes just like her dad. The children's rooms were all different in color. We wanted it to be different, so that they wouldn't want to get confused. I would sit with them at night and tell them stories. He taught his kids, the good from the bad, and how to be a great person in life. He also said to be strong, be kind, and be honest. Everything will be well. That evening we were served potage. We had it at the dining hall as always, we enjoyed the potage. It was good on cold nights. It's like we were kids again. Me and Walt looked at each other and smiled. After dinner, we went outside on the balcony overlooking at the view. "I love looking at the stars at night." Said Margery. That night it looked like there was diamonds in the sky. "You look beautiful tonight, Margery" "It's getting cold outside; you're going to catch a cold." He wrapped his jacket, around her shoulders. And she smiled at Walt. For it was a beautiful night. "Let's retire for the night." Said Walt. The next morning, I had Genevieve and Melinda come to my chambers and decided to go for a walk outside on the grounds. I had told them that. They are my pride and joy in my life. We are close as sisters can be. The laugh's that we've have and the times that we shared have been the best times in my life. We walked outside and hugged each other. The next day someone knocked, and Thea and Giacomo came in and said, "we are so happy for everyone, it was a great wedding." "Sire, we are going to travel in the next few days, we will be visiting Rouen." Said Giacomo. "We have family there and want to stop and visit." The king said, "Take your time, when you come back, we have a surprise for the family." They packed their belongings, and the carriage was ready. There luggage's, were put on the carriage. The King and Queen waved goodbye to them both. They started their journey singing together in the carriage, and Giacomo held Thea's hand and that's when the carriage gets derailed. They lose their luggage on their way. The king gets word that Giacomo is hurt. "Jax!" the king calls. "Get the men, hurry and get the horses, and ride through the forest. Where they were going." Jax arrives and the carriage went in a ditch.

Thea is crying. And Giacomo is on the floor. Jax see's if he is still breathing. He comes close to him, "Don't worry Thea he will be fine." "He is still breathing." "Jax and his men wrap him and transported him on the new carriage." "Men, 1,2,3 lift." "He is in the carriage. We will follow him all the way to Rouen." We arrived at the family home, and Thea runs towards her aunt and uncle. "Call the doctor!" Thea said to Madame Blanche. Thea told everyone to come in. They put Giacomo, on a bed. He opened his eyes. The doctor came in and said, "His rib is broken." "But he will be fine in a few days." "Thank you doctor." Madame Blanche said. Thea took Giacomo's hand and said, "Darling you will be fine, and I love you." The days went by, and he got up on his feet. He recovered nicely. Thea's aunt said, "Now we can enjoy Rouen." Madame Blanche said, "We'll take the carriage around." and Thea and Giacomo got in. Rouen. The town was always the same. A beautiful place. Cobblestone streets, and the friendly people with their smile always to greet everyone. The smell of hot bread baking at the shops and the pastry shops with their desserts. We walked in and took a few cakes to my aunt's home. We walked on the streets of Rouen, and it felt like home. That night we had supper at the ballroom. Everyone was there, we celebrated to good health, and that Giacomo is back on his feet. Madame

Blanche, and her husband Monsieur Paul were happy and raised their glasses too. Everyone said, "Oui, Oui." The men drank. We all celebrated together that night. When the celebrations ended, we went back to our chambers. Thea said to Giacomo, "I love you." And Giacomo said, "I love you too to Thea." They kissed and went to bed. The next day my aunt said to me, "I have a surprise for you. Thea, we decided to give you and Giacomo some of our lands and homes." "You will be called Madame Thea, and Giacomo will be Comte Giacomo from now on. As your sister has titled so shall you." She didn't know what to say. "Thank you, my aunt, and uncle." She said. "It's nothing." Said Madame Blanche. "We are ready to go back home." Thea said. We got in the carriage and headed back home. We passed through the green forest, with beautiful flowers blooming on our way home. We noticed; the birds were chirping. Like a sign, to welcome us home. Once we arrived home, the king and Queen were there to greet us. "Welcome home Madame Thea and Comte Giacomo." The gates opened and we walked in. We walked into our chambers, and we told the servants to prepare a basin for Comte Giacomo and Madame Thea. After there long trip home. The next day, the King and his men went out at the tavern. He invited all his first officer's men. We rode to the tavern; it wasn't too far off a trip. When we arrived, we dismounted our horses and tied them and walked in. We were greeted with an applause at the tavern. For everyone knew that Giacomo was ok. And that the men and women were married. Comte Vance and Comte Ferand were with us. And Comte Vance said, "Ale to everyone!" and Comte Fernand said, "Yes! More ale for everyone." They cheered. We sat down, and they brought us fresh chicken, potatoes and ale. We ate and then started making jokes. The men loved my jokes. Her is one, the king said. "If one chicken crosses over the fence and gets caught. What do you call it? Fence hen." They all laughed loud. "Come bring more ale!" They kept on joking and laughing. "Come, someone say a joke or sing something." The king asked. They all started to sing a song. That afternoon, we had a great time. Then we had to head home. I paid the tavern and got ready to head back. We were a little drunk, but we mounted our horses, and we laughed all the way. The gates were opened, and we went in. The Queen said, "Walt you're in a great mood. Did you have a great time at the tavern with your men? I see you have a great grin on your face." "Yes, Margey we had a great time, with the men. Especially me with my jokes." The King said. Later that night, the Queen asked the maid to draw a bath for the King. The King went to his chambers and got in the basin. The next day, The King and Queen went down for breakfast. There was poached eggs, cheese and fresh bread. They also had a cup of tea. He leaned over, and kissed Margery, "You look beautiful today, as always my Queen." Said the King. "And you, my King look handsome today." Margery said. Now William is 17 years old. "How the years went by." The King said. "Let's play chess." The Queen said. It was raining outside. "Tell the servants to call the children to play chess." The servants called the children to come down and play chess. They came down one by one, down the grand staircase. They sat down and started to play chess. They laughed and enjoyed the evening. While the children were playing, Margery walked towards the glass-stained windows, and saw the snow fall. She smiled and said to the servants, "We will start Christmas preparations around the castle." The servants said, "Yes, your highness." They went to the ballroom and started taking decorations out. They started to decorate the windows, the railing of the grand staircase all in red. There was pottery with branches of pine, that smelled through the air. It looked splendid. After the chess game, the children went to the ballroom. They were excited for Christmas. Every year at the castle, it was a big event. The children said to the servant, "Can you make us cookies of joy for tomorrow?" and they said, "Of course." That evening they decorated the ballroom, beautifully. They went to their chambers, and everyone went to bed. The next morning, they smelled the fresh baked cookies. "Wow!" the children said. As the cookies were placed on a plate for the children, and for us too. We ate the cookies, with milk. Then the children played in the snow.

# Chapter 8
## A New Member Arrives

That evening, everyone was informed that a celebration would take place. Everyone in the ballroom was organized and ready. The king had a surprise, for everyone. We all got dressed up and entered the ballroom. It looked magnificent. All lit up and ready for the King and Queen to enter. When the King and Queen entered, they said everyone look at the corner of the room. There was a table, and on it there were gifts for everyone. And the king said, "The gifts are from,…" The doors opened. There stands a tall handsome man, and he walked in with Colette. "Everyone, this is my nephew Prince Constantine, welcome him home." Everyone clapped and said "welcome home". His mom started to cry, he spoke and said, "A little token, from my family." "Thank you everyone." Prince Constantine said. The music started to play, and everyone went to greet the prince. He was very happy. They all started to dance. The king asked him. "How was your trip?" "It was a good voyage." He replied. "My dad left me land, and homes, but my new start will be here." "Your quarters are ready, and welcome home." said the king. Prince Constantine, mingled with the crowd and he danced with some ladies. After a few drinks, he said, "Goodnight to everyone in the room." The party ended on a high note. Everyone liked their gift and took it to their chambers. Some got necklaces, others got brooches, and some got gold crosses. The next morning, we got up, me and Walt. Took a breath of fresh air outside. It was a beautiful morning. The sun was out. Me and William took a walk on the grounds. "Come my son," said Walt. "Your cousin Prince Constantine is here, we will have breakfast at the dining room, this morning." Said the king. "We will later go horseback riding." Said Willam. Margery smiled too. Prince Constantine entered the room, he greeted everyone, and he smiled at William. "Hello cousin, how have you been." Willam said. "I have been great." He answered. "Come sit, have breakfast." Willam said. They sat that morning and enjoyed their meal. Once they finished breakfast, they headed to the stables. "Let's go for that ride cousin." Willam said. "Like old times." Prince Constantine said. They rode through the forest, with snow blowing through their hair. Laughing, and they enjoyed the afternoon. Walt looked at her. "Come here." He said. And he kissed her lips. She couldn't stop kissing him. She kept on looking in his eyes. "Stop" he would say, joking to her. "Bonjour, my Queen." And he kissed her again. "Bonjour my King." Margery said. And they laughed. They got up and headed to their chamber. He grabbed her waist and kissed her again. She laughed again. He said to her, "You are so beautiful." He grabbed her and made love to her. She said in his ear, "I'm so happy." "You are my love now and always." They kissed each other. They got the servants, to fill the basin with warm water. They took their bath and got dressed. They started their day and walked together hand in hand. They got to the kitchen, and asked the cook to serve them eggs, and bread out of the oven. They sat and smiled to each other. They decided to go see Prince Constantine, if everything was alright. And he said "Yes, my quarters are fine, and the food is great Sire." "Now today I will ride my horse, Common." "That's great." said the King. He took his horse out and they rode through the forest. His white horse galloped, and they rode as one. Constantine was so happy. He rode his horse through the wind. He loved riding and after he said to Common. "Let's go home, good boy." He rode slowly to the stables. As he brought his horse, he saw a beautiful woman near the stables, with long red hair. He asked her name,

"My name is Emma Josephine." she said, "What a beautiful name." he said. "I'm staying here in Court." He said. She smiled, "I'm happy you're here." He left the horse to rest, while he washed his boots. He cleaned himself up and took a hot bath. He dressed up and went to the dining area. He asked the cooks to prepare breakfast, and the smell from the kitchen took over. He couldn't wait to eat. And then the food came. He thanked the cooks and started eating. Once he finished, he left the dining area. He decided to take a nap, before supper. Later that evening the king said, "We will all have a meeting so that are nephew will take over some duties." The meeting took place, he was happy so were we. The next morning, Price Constantine took a walk on the grounds near the town. He went in town to see what was new in town. While he was walking. He sees Emma Josephine, with two other girls walking. I approached her and said, "Hi Emma Josephine. Would you like to have dinner tonight at the castle with me." "Yes." She said. Her friends were so happy for her. That night, the king asked the servants to prepare the dinning room. The King was informed that Prince Constantine, had invited someone for dinner. The tables were set, with fresh flowers. We sat at the table, and she was announced, "Emma Josephine is here." She said, "Thank you for having me here your majesty." As she walked through the doors, we all staired at her for she had the reddish hair and is very pretty. Prince Constantine walked towards her, she curtsied and took her hand. He escorted her to the table. They ate a roast, with potatoes with a nice glass of wine. And everyone had a good evening. The King asked to Emma Josephine, if she would like to join us for Christmas dinner. "Yes, your highness I will attend." She said. Prince Constantine looked at her and said. "I'm so happy that you will be here." After dinner, he escorted Emma Josephine to her carriage. "I'll see you soon at Christmas dinner, here." He kissed her hand, and said, "My name is Prince Constantine." She smiled and said, "I'm honored." She smiled. "The carriages will come to you up tomorrow night."

Christmas day came. The preparations were ready, lanterns were lit all over the castle, and music was playing. The guests were on their way. Prince Willam said to Prince Constantine, "My cousin you met a beautiful lady." "Yes." He said. "I want her for my wife." Said Prince Constantine. Prince Willam, smiled. He said to his cousin. "I'm happy for you." The evening began, Colette walked in with a beautiful blue gown with her hair pined up. With Prince Constantine. Margery walked in with a red beautiful gown with her crown on her head. As beautiful as always, with the King and her children. The doors opened, and Emma Joesphine walked in. She had a beautiful green dress, with a pearl necklace around her neck. She walked in with her friend beside her. "Welcome lady Emma Joesphine and lady Mabel." They greeted and curtsied to the King and Queen. "Ladies and gentlemen, raise your glass this is a Christmas celebration for everyone here! God bless our family!" "Cheers everyone." They raised their glass and cheered. They ate dinner, everyone danced, they laughed, music was playing. Prince Constantine asked lady Emma Josephine to dance. And Prince William asked, lady Mabel to dance. The evening was splendid.

# Chapter 9
## The Next Generation

Fast forward in years. We were proud of our family. They are the next generation. Victoria hugged her sister every day. They were close. Thea and Victoria went for a walk on the grounds. With the sun shining that day. They walked and talked. Victoria said to Thea, "You are the best sister I could have. I don't know what I would have done, if something happened to you." Thea answered back and said, "I love you now and always, you are my sister always." They hugged each other and walked back to the castle. And said, "Let's go sneak in the kitchen and we will steal some cake." We tip toed in and were laughing all the way. They ran fast upstairs into their courters, saying to one another, "remember the time we did this with the Queen." "She is a beautiful lady, we still laughed together with the Queen. And talk about it." The years have passed, but the memories stayed in our hearts. Then one night, me and Walt went for a walk. It was cold out, and he grabbed my hand and held me tight. We looked at the stars together and he said, "We had had a great life, and our children are grown, and you are my wife first. And my Queen. I have loved you from the moment I first saw you." The King said. "I loved you from the moment I saw you." She said. We went inside and I started to cough. The days that followed it got worst. The doctor came in and told Walt she won't last the night. He started to cry, and he didn't want her to know. I held her hand, I said to Margery "I will always love you, in this life and the next." He tells her. "Remember these words." "I will love you for life and never forget these words." "We will reunite in a thousand years." "I know" she said. She took her last breath, and she was gone. He buried her with her ring on her finger. Written, "Love you for life." On the ring. Her two sisters were buried beside her with initials on their ring, that said, "Forever sisters." Walt dies a few months later. Willam buries his father. Everyone stands still. William puts his father's crown on his tomb. And said, "He was a king at heart, and soul my father the King."

Everyone cried after the burial. We held each other and started heading back to the castle. Heading back home, Prince Willam was going to become the new King. We rode with the women in the carriages.

The bells were ringing and the people in the town gathered to pay respect for the King. I said to myself, my family is in good hands as I will be the next king. We arrived at the gates. The attendants were all waiting for us. One attendant said, "Sire, may I speak." "Yes, you may." He answered. "We will miss your father and his wife the Queen. But you will be a strong king as your father was. I am honored, to be of service to this beautiful family." I answered him back and said, "Thank you." "You are appreciated in this home." "Everyone tonight, we shall be at the chapel for a night of silence." "Yes, Sire." Everyone answered. I walked into my chamber and cried. I had a glass of wine. I knew I was responsible from now on, and in everything I do. I went to the throne room and sat in my father's chair. I felt his presence. "I will make you proud." I said to myself. I ordered the staff to prepare a dinner, just before the service for the chapel. I had Prince Constantine summoned. He arrived at the throne room and bowed his head. I said, "You're my cousin first and you will be by my side always from now on. You can address me as William." He hugged me and said "I will protect and honor everything here. We are cousins by blood, and our fathers would want us to rule and be proud." We hugged each other. "Yes cousin, have a glass of wine because our future is here.

# Chapter 10
## A New Life

The next morning, William gets up. He gets ready for breakfast. He calls Prince Constantine to join him, and his commander Jax. "How is married life Jax?" Prince Constantine said. "Married life is great. Thank you." Jax said. "How is Common, from his bruise?" Prince William said. "He recovered, and he is fine." Prince Constantine said. "Let's eat our breakfast. Willam ask the men to go hunting in the afternoon." "ok" said Jax. They ate their breakfast. It was a sunny day. The men gathered and mounted their horses and prepared for their day." "let's Catch pheasants." Jax said. It was a great day, to catch and gather food. "I got four!" Jax said. "Let's mount them on the horse. Let's give it to the cooks, and we will have it for dinner tonight." Jax said. We were so happy to head back home, so the cooks can clean them. We can have it for dinner tonight. The men gathered their tools. And headed back on their horse and headed back home. "Ladies, we gathered some pheasants for tonight." "It's going to be a great feast." Said Jax. "We can't wait. Let's tell the cooks." Said Madame Victoria. They called the cooks to gather them in the entrance to have them cooked. they were happy. "Tonight, we have a celebration." Prince Constantine said. "We will have the food for dinner, just before the coronation." "I will call everyone to gather for this great evening tonight." "I will also tell the cooks to prepare a surprise for everyone." said Prince Constantine. The ladies headed to their chambers, to get ready for a beautiful night. The maids did their hair. They put on beautiful gowns with beautiful shoes. The men got dressed as well. The maids prepared the dinning room, with fresh flowers, beautiful candles, and lanterns. They sounded the horn, and Prince William enters the room. They all applauded. everyone clapped. "Ladies and gentlemen, we are gathered here for Prince William to be crowned King." Prince Constantine said. They all raised their glass. "Tomorrow is going to be a great day." He said. They feasted and enjoyed the evening. Prince Elias went to Prince William to speak with him for a moment. "Prince Willam, after the coronation, I'll be leaving town for a few months, and I shall return." Said Prince Elias. "Whatever you need, I will have it ready for you." Prince Willaim said. Music was playing, people were dancing. The evening was great. The maids prepared the surprise, for the king. The gesture came in at the ballroom, and announced "Sire, here is your surprise." When the doors opened, and tall white icing cake came in.

Everyone was in awe. On the cake, there was a crown. With chocolate icing. They reeled it close to the future King. He stood up, and the maid said, "Our first slice goes to our beloved King." They clapped. He said, "Everyone enjoy a piece of cake." The festivities ended in a high note. They all gathered and had a great evening. We then were very tired and went to our chambers for the night. The next day, the sun was shinning at my window. As I looked outside, I noticed the carriages coming around. Today I was going to be King. Everyone in town were placing fresh flowers and throwing flowers in the streets. I started to get ready. The maids came in and dressed me, with a black suit with gold finishings on the collar, and a white shirt underneath. That morning, I told the maids, "Can you bring in my father's sword." "Yes Sire." They curtsied and left the room. The music was playing outside, people were gathering around the castle. They were all excited for what is going to happen next.

I passed by Prince Constantine's chamber. He was ready in his finest clothes. His brother was dressed and ready as well. My family came down the staircase. All dressed for all eyes to see. Jax, Marcus and Joah was beside as I strolled to the gates. The carriages were ready. Jonah said, "Sire, are you ready." I answered back, "Now I know how my father felt on his day of coronation." The doors opened, we walked towards the carriages. We went on the carriages. The people rejoiced with excitement. The people all applauded outside.

The Carriages passed by them. They waved at the future King. The carriages stopped in front of the cathedral. They all got inside and took there seats. I was the last one in. I was nervous, but very happy and looking forward to being King. I walked in and everyone applauded. I kneeled down, and the bishop took my father's sword. And placed it on my shoulder.

He repeated these words

*"From this day, will you promise and swear to protect the people and the town in this country?"*

*"Yes I will." answered the King.*
*"I stand here and I give you King William.*

*"Everyone started cheering. "Long live the King."*

They walked out of the cathedral. Everyone clapped at the great King. He went on his carriage and headed through the town. While everyone was shouting in excitement through the streets. The white carriage and white horses were spectacular to watch. They headed through town. He opened the drape and waved at the crowd.

The carriages arrived at the gate. Colette was the first to congratulate the King. She whispered. "Your parents would have been proud." "I have Witnessed an amazing day." Colette said. He smiled And said, "Thank you Colette." The maids had prepared the whole castle to its splendor. There was flowers, candles and beautiful lanterns everyone, throughout The castle. The smell of food throughout the halls. It was splendid. They couldn't wait to begin the feast.

They gathered all in, towards the banquet. For a big celebration. Everyone arrived and took their seats. The iron beautiful doors opened. The King enters with his family, while the people cheered. All eyes were on him. He went towards the table, where his King chair is placed. Where a gold goblet is handed to him. While he gives his speech. "From this day forward, I shall protect this town. This country, the towns, and people. For I am your King." Everyone raised their glass and said, "God bless the King."

They clapped and cheered and sat at their seats for dinner. The maids rolled in five roasted geese, with fresh potatoes, vegetables, and fresh breads with garlic for the court. They dinned, they danced and laughed for the gesture had come in to say some jokes.

Jax raises his glass, and says "To a great man, just like your father was. May you be blessed with whatever your heart desires. To the King." Jax said. The women picked up their gowns, and grabbed their men, and started dancing. The music took over. Some people laughed, drank and chatted among themselves. It was a great night.

# Chapter 11
## A New Beginning for Prince Elias

The next morning, they cleared out the banquet hall. The maids put all the drapes away in their cabinets. They stored their candles, and went on their way to the kitchen. The cooks started preparing breakfast. They were making funnel cake. With strawberries and apples. Which they took the apples from the tree from their garden. The maids picked up the apples in the morning, And started preparing the cake. The King woke up, And he knocked at Prince Elias door. "Prince Elias, the food is ready, were going to have breakfast. I told the servants to prepare your carriage for your departure." "Thank you, Sire." Prince Elias said. We all met at the dinning room. Everyone joined us. Prince Constantine sat beside his brother, and said, "If there Is anything you need, just summon me. I'm at your disposal." They ate breakfast. The fresh boiled eggs, were amazing. The best part was the fennel cake. It arrived with fresh strawberries and apples on a beautiful gold platter which was put on the center of the table as we ate. "This looks delicious. My, my, your cooks are amazing." Prince Elias said.

Prince Elias, says "As you know, I have packed for my voyage. I shall be back in a few months. God willing. I'll be going to Reims, for a few months and I shall return." "Brother, are you going back to castle to check on things in Reims?" said Prince Constantine. "Brother, if there is anything you need, I'll be here." He said. "Thank you, brother." Prince Elias said. Later he took his luggage that he prepared for his voyage, and started to head out the door. He says, "Bye brother, I will see you again soon." He goes to his carriage and started going to Reims. They took two days to arrive. The coachmen, brings Prince Elias to his hometown Reims They arrived at the castle gates. He opens the carriage, and the servants are greeting him At the door. "Welcome home Prince Elias." They said. "Thank you, I will be in my chambers if you need me, I am very tired from the voyage." He said. They said "How was the coronation?" "The coronation was splendid. It went very well. I am very happy for my cousin." "He became King." Prince Elias said. "Good news! We are so happy for him. Give him the news from us, when you

Go back." The servant said.

Prince Elias walked into his room. And rested on his bed. He told the maids, to prepare a bath for him. Just before dinner. The maids started preparing the basin, with warm water. As soon it was ready, they summon Prince Elias for his bath. The maids started cooking for dinner. They made roasted chicken, and vegetables with a glass of wine waiting for him. He took his bath and was well groomed. He was ready for dinner. They unpacked his belongings in his room. He was summoned for dinner. He went downstairs, and the servants came in and brought him his food. He sat at the table and started eating. The food was delicious. He ate dinner and went to bed.

The next morning, he headed out in the courtyard and asked the servants to pick up the leaves outside and what needs to be done. "Yes, sire." The servant said. As I was looking down the road a carriage is coming up on the road which I've never seen before. The horses had beautiful feathers on their hair. The lady looked beautiful. The coachmen stopped the carriage, right in front of me. She moves the drape from the carriage, and says "Monsieur, who are you? I've been here for months, and I never seen anyone from here?" she said. "My name is Prince Elias, and my father lived here." She was startled. "I'm sorry

Monsieur to not have known." "It is alright." Prince Elias said. "May I ask your name?" She replied "Countess Mabel Lucia." He kissed her hand. "It is my pleasure to meet you." He said. She blushed. And returned a smile. She headed back home. He continued his orders to his servants outside. He couldn't stop thinking of her. They removed the plants and brought them in the castle. The servants cleaned the front of the castle, and I said, "Once you are finished you can go rest." He said to the servants. He walked back in and went towards the courtyard to get some fresh air. The maids got him a glass of wine for the evening. He drank his wine, Looking at the fountains in the courtyard. "What a Beautiful night." He said. The next morning, he decided to head into town. He called the coachman to get the carriage to bring him to town. They prepared The carriage, and they brought him to town. He walked around to see what was going on in town. He noticed one couple talking. They were talking about Countess Mabel Lucia's aunt had passed away. That she is taking charge of the aunts castle. He overheard this. Now he knows she is wealthy. He interrupts the couple talking and said, "May I know where she staying?" They turned around

"Prince Elias, are you back in town?" they said. "Yes, I am for a short Visit." They bowed. "Yes, Sire.

She is living near the bakery, just before your home." She said.

He was amazed.

"The bakery Sire, needs some funds. To get new tools." They said. "Thank you for letting me know. It shall be done." He said.

"Thank you both. Have a good day." Prince Elias said.

That evening, he took his carriage and road near the bakery. He walked in and gave them coins for new tools. They were so happy. "Thank you Sire." He left with a smile. He headed home, and his servant said "Sire, we received a invitation, for you." "I shall read it." said Prince Elias. "Thank you." He walks towards the dining hall and opens the note. It is a mask ball. From Countess Mabel Lucia. He is stunned. He called the servant back. He tells the servant. "I will reply to the invitation that I shall attend. I put my seal on the envelope, please return it the countess." Prince Elias said. "Yes, Sire." The servant answered. Later That evening they were preparing his clothes, for the ball in a few days time. He asked the servant, "I'll be going to town tomorrow, to get a mask." That night, He rested and went to bed. The next morning, he wakes up, has breakfast. He is looking forward to going to town. They prepared him boiled eggs and fresh bread. He dressed up, and combed his hair and headed to town. The carriages were ready. He headed to town and goes to a shop. He found a mask for the ball. They wrapped it in a beautiful gold cloth. As he is walking out the door, Countess Mabel Lucia arrives as he is walking out. "Hello, Prince Elias. How are you today?" "I'm good today, I just picked up my mask for your ball." She replied "May I see it? Sire" she said. He shows her the mask.

It was in gold and black. "I shall wear a black and gold dress that evening at the ball." He smiled. He was looking at her beautiful smile and gorgeous red hair. She looked stunning, in her black cape. "May, I ask you a question Countess?" said Prince Elias. "Yes, you may." she said. "Can I see you tomorrow at my castle for lunch? We shall dine together." She smiled and said "Yes, I'll be there Prince Elias, see you then." She smiled and left. Morning came, he woke up and started his day. The sun was glaring through the room, and he dressed up and headed downstairs. The breakfast was made and he asked the cooks to prepare a delicious meal for lunch for we have a guest. "I need you to prepare for me a meal for lunch, for i have a guest arriving at lunch, not any guest she is a countess." "Please have fresh flowers and candles lit. thank you." They curtsied and started preparing the meal For lunch. He had his breakfast and he headed for his father's chambers. The room was filled of his father's belongings. One thing stood out. His father's necklace. He had it cleaned, and he will wear it for this occasion. The servants started preparing the dining hall.

They placed fresh flowers, with candles. That lit up the whole castle. They had nice drapes in the dinning room. The cooks were preparing the meal. Everything was in place. There was a knock on the door.

The servant opened the door. The countess Mabel Lucia arrived. She looked stunning. She was wearing a gold and green dress, her hair was pinned beautifully as she entered.

"Sire, the countess is here." As he walked towards Her. She looked beautiful. He looked at her and said "Welcome to my home, countess. You look beautiful." "Thank you." she replied. "Let's go to the dining hall." She walked in and said "What a beautiful room." "The food smells great." she said. "I will like to court You" Prince Elias said. She replied, "I feel the same way." she smiled. He gave her a glass of wine, and picked up his goblet and said, "Cheers to us." He started asking her questions about her family. "Do you have any other siblings?" he said. "Yes, Sire. I have one sister. She is a bit older than me." "what about you?" and he answers back "I have one brother older then me." They talked that night and they went for a stroll on the grounds. "May I hold your hand?" he said. She replied "Yes you may." The evening ended. The servants escorted her back home. He told her "When will I see you again." "In a few days you shall come to my home." The next few days, went very quickly he received a note, from Prince Constantine, if everything is alright. I replied "Everything, is well at home. I am Courting someone. You will meet her soon. Brother." he sealed the envelope and sent it back to Prince Constantine. The servant tells Prince Elias that Countess Mabel Lucia has invited him for supper tonight, at her home.

The carriage gets ready for Prince Elias to go to Countess Mabel Lucia home. Once he arrives at the gates, her servant brings him to the dinning hall. As he enters the dinning hall, he marveled at the white columns and beautiful artifacts in the room. She had nice drapes in here castle. As I am looking at this she enters the Room. With her long red hair, with a black and red dress. He bowed to her. They were escorted to there seats for dinner. They had lamb with vegetables. They were laughing together and drinking wine. It was a beautiful night. They went outside on the terrace, and looked at the stars. "I'll be seeing you at the ball." she said. "I can't wait." Prince Elias said. The next couple of days, the ballroom was getting set up for the big event. He got up that morning, he went for his morning walk. He asked the maids, to prepare him a bath and to prepare his clothes for the ball. The maid got his clothes on his bed, and with his mask ready for him. He took his bath, and was groomed. The carriage was prepared, and he made his way towards her castle. There was so many people arriving. It was spectacular to see everything lit and people dressed in costumes. I just couldn't wait to see her.

## Chapter 12
### A Big Surprise

As I am walking in. I hear music playing, people dancing and people drinking. As I start to walk towards the hallway, towards the ballroom. They said, "stop the music, everyone look at the staircase." "Countess Mabel Lucia." Is announced. She had a beautiful black and gold dress with a long train. Her mask was in gold and black. Her beautiful hair was pinned up. She wore a red ruby necklace around her neck. She looked stunning. "Welcome to the ball everyone, and enjoy the evening." Everyone clapped and everyone cheered. She walked down the White marble staircase with her long train that followed. As she got to the last step. Prince Elias took her arm, and asked for a dance. They played soft music and everyone stared. "What a beautiful couple." They said. They danced the night. The food was delicious. All sorts of food was displayed on the tables. with wine, ale and beer. Her sister was there and asked her "Who is this man?" she replied "Prince Elias." "oh, what a handsome man sister." She said. "Prince Elias this is my sister." he bowed and said "what a pleasure to meet you."

The gesture recited poems for the rest of the evening everyone had a great time at the ball. The people started leaving, it was getting late. There was only me and Mabel left on the dance floor. I grabbed her waist and kissed her. She was fluttered. He said "I have a surprise for you." "I want you to be my wife. I will give you this token, for my mother wore this on her wedding day as a symbol of my love to you." She kissed him back. She couldn't wait for the wedding day. "I love you Mabel." Prince Elias said. "I love you Elias." Said Mabel. They kissed one more time. He said To her, "I'll introduce you to my brother once we get married." The night ended. They walked hand in hand towards the door, until he got on his carriage and road off. The next morning, he asked all the attendance to be present for the good news. He said "I have found my wife, and I will marry her in a month from now.

Preparations will start here. And I shall return back with my wife, for them to meet my brother and my cousin." The servants curtsied and were happy with the news. In the next few weeks, the preparations started at the castle everything, was in place. There were bouquets of fresh flowers, beautiful draperies in silk, and a gift for his new bride. The people gathered around the castle. The celebration started.

The announcement was made, that the wedding will take place in two nights. The next day, it was a lovely morning. Prince Elias had an idea. He started his day, with breakfast in the dinning hall. He had fresh eggs, with a morning pie.

It was delicious. He ate it all. I'll tell my servants I'll be going to town. "Joseph, can you prepare my carriage please. I'll be going to the market in town." "Ok." said Joseph. He got his cape, with his fathers gold chain. He opened the iron doors, and the carriage was waiting for him. He rode through the village with leaves falling winter was here. As the carriage stopped I walked in at the jewellers.

I asked the jewellers to have something done for Mabel. The jewellers shows him what he has, and he falls in love with this beautiful ring that he has. He asked her, if they can put initials on this ring. "This is a unique ring, I will put the initials on the ring, to my love M-L." said the merchant. "Of course, Sire, it will be beautiful." He asked for her to put it in a beautiful cloth. "Can this be done for tomorrow?" Prince Elias said. "It can be done." The merchant said. "Tomorrow I will have someone pick up the ring." said Prince Elias.

He leaves the merchant, and gets back on his carriage, and heads home. He arrives at the castle. He is so happy for the news that the ring will be ready. She will love it. She sends a note to Countess Mabel Lucia for her to join him for dinner tonight. He walks in the castle, he tells the servant "I invited Countess Mabel Lucia for dinner tonight. Please prepare something delicious for us tonight." Prince Elias said. "Sire, it will be our pleasure tonight." The servants bowed and left.

The maids went in the garden to get fresh flowers for the evening. They placed it in a beautiful vase on the center of the table. The cooks were preparing the meal. The meal was beef pies with vegetables. And for dessert they had cheesecake with fresh fruits. I asked the maid to pick me out an outfit for tonight. The maids picked out a black and gold outfit for the evening. They groomed him for this occasion. He was happy for tonight, for he would see Countess Mabel Lucia. There was a knock on the door. It was Countess Mabel Lucia. "Sire we have the Countess here." He ran down the stairs, and said "My dear, You look so beautiful tonight." Prince Elias said. "My handsome Prince you look great as well." Countess Mabel Lucia said. The cooks said, "The food is ready." They made there way through the dining room, where they saw fresh flowers at the center of the table. "This is so beautiful." She said.

"Tonight, we will have beef pies, with vegetables. And for dessert we will have a cheesecake." She was happy. "I love cheesecake. Cheesecake is my favorite dessert." said Countess Mabel Lucia. "I will go get the wine." The servant said. As the servant left. He asked her for a kiss. she smiled and kissed him. The beef pies arrived. The smell was so wonderful. The countess Mabel Lucia said, "this looks delightful. I can't wait to eat this." We ate our meals. Laughed and had our wine. He said, "My darling, tomorrow is our wedding day." Prince Elias said. "I cannot wait." she said. "let's go for a stroll outside." Said prince Elias. "It's a little chilly tonight." He grabbed his cape, and wrapped it around her shoulders. He said, "This will keep you warm." She smiled at him. "Thank you darling." They walked on the grounds. They stopped right in front of the fountains, and he whispered in her ear. "You are the love of my life." she answered back. "Your mine too." They started to head back to the castle. The maid came out, "Sire, the cheesecake is ready." "Thank you, Camille. We will have it now." Prince Elias said. They smiled. We ate the dessert near the fireplace. The fire was lit. it looked wonderful. As we sat Together and ate the cheesecake, she looked beautiful. "I can't wait to have her for my wife." The night came To a close. I kissed her good night, for tomorrow is a big day for us." The carriage came around. I kissed her good night. "Tomorrow we will be husband and wife." she said. "Yes, we will." He answered. "Sweet dreams darling." The carriage rode off.

## Wedding of Prince Elias and Countess Mabel Lucia 1251

That morning, she woke up and went to have her breakfast. After her meal she headed to her chamber. Her Dress was layed out on her bed. It was a long, beautiful white dress. She had a pearl necklace to wear with it, with beautiful shoes. They put on her dress, with her jewelry and her shoes. She looked stunning. She got on her carriage, and they rode her to the castle. When she arrived, they dismounted the carriage.

The servant said, "Everyone be at the ballroom, and the Ceremony will take place." She walked in the castle, with her long gown in the castle, with her long train. As the people watched, she arrived towards Prince Elias. The bishop was there, he handed her a ring. He placed it on her finger. The bishop said, "You are men and wife." The crowd cheers for them and they walked to the ballroom, where music played and the people greeted them both. They danced through the night. Prince Elias and his wife, danced one last dance. He kissed her and everyone cheered. The music ended and everyone retired in there courters.

The maids prepared their bed. Prince Elias helped her undress, because the dress was heavy. I helped her undress, and I whispered in her ear, "I have found, the perfect women. Your beauty and smile captured my heart from the moment I saw you." she answered back "You are a perfect man for me, when I first saw you."

They kissed and fell asleep in each others arms.

The next morning, the snow was falling. Prince Elias rode his horse just before breakfast. While Princess Mabel, tour the grounds and saw him riding his horse. He waved at me and I waved back. "I'll be there in a few minutes." She smiled and went back inside. That morning, they had breakfast when he came back from his ride. "Good morning my wife." Prince Elias said. "How are you today?" she smiled and said. "I'm very happy today my handsome husband." They walked hand in hand. They entered the dining room and had breakfast. The day passed quickly. before we knew it. It was nighttime. We decided to sit near the fire, and the maids brought us cookies and tea. It was a beautiful evening.

Morning came, the maids were summoned to fill the basin with warm water with jasmine for Princess Mabel. As they entered, she went in the basin to take her bath. While Prince Elias did the same. They finished their baths and they had dried her. The maids helped her dress in a red gown. He got dressed in his black suit, as they walked into the dinning hall. While the maids placed boiled eggs, fresh fruits, and cheese on the table. They couldn't stop looking at each other. "This food looks splendid." she told the maids. They smiled. "Thank you, Princess Mabel." The servant said as they curtsied. We finished breakfast, and we headed to the terrace for a breath of fresh air. Prince Elias kissed her neck. You know, we shall return home, so that my family, will meet you. They are having a ball just for us to attend." "yes, I know." She answered. "Tomorrow we can leave and travel back to my home." "Yes, my darling we shall leave in the morning." Princess Mabel said. The fresh air felt wonderful standing there with my beautiful wife. I never been so happy in my live. They walked back inside. Prince Elias said. "I'll see you in our Chamber. I need to have the servants know about us Leaving in the morning." "yes" she said. "I'll see you in our chamber." Princess Mabel said.

Prince Elias went to speak with the servant, to have the carriage ready in the morning. "We shall travel back home to see my brother," "yes sire, the carriage will be ready." The servant said. I went back to our courters and we started to pack. "I shall be so happy to meet your family." Princess Mabel said. "I can't wait to introduce you as my wife." said Prince Elias. They kissed. He grabbed her close to him. "I love You." He said. "I love you too." she said. "Let's finish packing, and let's get something to eat for supper." Prince Elias said. The servant summoned Prince Elias "Sire, the food is ready." They went to the dining hall and ate supper with his wife Princess Mabel. They were seated at the table. The servant served them wine and the maid came in with fresh roasted chicken with herbs, and potatoes."

Prince Elias said "I love chicken with those potatoes, that Were made with rosemary." I too drank my wine, as I made a toast to my beautiful wife.

"To my beautiful wife, which I love dearly. May we cherish these years together, as we take this rode together, as a couple."

They toasted and drank. She smiled.

We were finishing our meal. The servant said, "Prince Elias. It's a great night for a stroll. If you and your wife would like to go for a stroll in the gardens." "yes." Prince Elias answered. "While we will load the carriage with your belongings." The servant said. He held his hand to Princess Mabel and they walked past the white columns towards the beautiful iron gates and walked out, "What a beautiful evening." "Yes." said Princess Mabel. She looked up at the night sky, it was lit with stars, "Isn't it wonderful." Prince Mabel said. "Yes, it's beautiful." Prince Elias said. "A beautiful night with a beautiful wife, what more can I ask for." She kissed his soft lips, as they embraced each other. "Shall we return to our courters for tomorrow it will be a long journey." said Prince Elias. "yes." said Princess Mabel. They walked in, and started to go up the marble stairs, and go to our chambers. They fell asleep and morning came. They had boiled eggs, and a tarte for breakfast. They had their breakfast, and left Reims. The trip was long, and they had arrived. The carriage stopped, and she peeked out of the carriage, she was in shock. She recognized the castle. When Emma Josephine, brought her there once, but she didn't say anything at that moment. The coachmen, helped her dismount the carriage, and they did the same for Prince Elias. They marched in and went straight to there chambers. The coachmen brought their belongs. "I think we should unpack and rest for tonight." Prince Elias said. "At the ball, you will meet my family." "yes." said Princess Mabel. "I'm exhausted." She fell asleep on the bed. And so did he. After a few hours they woke up, and he asked the maids to prepare a hot bath for them both. The maids helped Princess Mabel in the basin. She said "Thank you to the maids." They curtsied. After 10 minutes, the maids came in, and helped Princess Mabel dress for the evening. She wore a blue velvet gown with gold around her sleeves. Her red hair was pinned for the occasion. The maids groomed him. They did his hair like he wanted it. He wore his white shirt, and a blue velvet jacket to match her. As they are descending the stairs, they were announced at the entrance door. The servants opened the doors, they entered, and Prince Elias says

"This is my wife Princess Mabel Lucia."

Everyone applauded. They were happy to see him back at court. King William is stunned. Because he notices it's Mabel. The same girl that he got introduced by Emma Josephine. He turns around and whispers to Prince Constantine's ear, "That's Mabel? I thought I would never see her again." said King William. Prince Constantine turns around, and whispers in William's ear, "I thought I would never see her again too. It's been months, that we haven't seen her. Who would of thought of seeing her again."

"In fact, here we are with your brother as his wife." King William said.

# Acknowledgments

It's a pleasure working with everyone at Tellwell. Thank you for making this dream a reality. Thanking my family, for their support. It means everything to me.

# Last word from the Author

Paris captured my heart with the cute
Shops that I visited. It stayed with me.
I wrote this story which takes Place in France.
There will be a second book in this story.
Merci tout le monde.
Thank you.

**Look for her other books online at amazon, or in stores!**

In stores and online

# Note from the Author

May the heaven shine on my king, is the first book of a series. Book 2 will be coming out soon!

www.ingramcontent.com/pod-product-compliance
Lightning Source LLC
LaVergne TN
LVHW041645060526
838200LV00040B/1727